THE EYES OF INNOCENCE

There was a faint sound behind her.

THE
EYES OF INNOCENCE

BY

MAURICE LEBLANC

WILDSIDE PRESS: MMIII

Published by
Wildside Press, LLC
P.O. Box 301
Holicong, PA 18928-0301 USA
www.wildsidepress.com

Wildside Press Edition: MMIII

CONTENTS

INTRODUCTION

by Darrell Schweitzer

Maurice Leblanc (1864-1941) was a French writer, born in Rouen, who studied for a law degree but dropped out of law school before settling in Paris and making his career as a fiction writer. His earliest works were critically praised but not especially popular. All this changed when his character Arsène Lupin appeared as a series of magazine stories in 1905. From this point on, his fortune was made, but rather like A. Conan Doyle with Sherlock Holmes, Leblanc found himself trapped by his own popularity. All the public wanted from him was more Lupin, about whom he ultimately wrote 24 volumes up through 1939, with a 25th only discovered in 2011 and published in 2012.

Lupin is, by any standard, a remarkable creation, a suave and witty master thief, who never harms anyone, but instead enjoys life to the fullest and perpetually thumbs his nose as authority figures, most notably his series nemesis, the relentless detective Ganimard. He may control a criminal network as large as that of Professor Moriarty, but he never seems particularly menacing. If one were to encounter Lupin, one would surely come away unharmed, but if one happened to be carrying a priceless jewel or a gold watch, it would just as surely prove to be missing. He only robs the very rich, scoundrels, or both.

For Lupin, crime is almost a sport. He has to keep most of what he steals to support his operations, but he might also return treasures on a whim. In one instance, he merely left his card behind with a note saying that he would return as soon as the antique furniture was authentic. His style and much of his personality may be summed up by a message he sends to the Baron Cahon:

> There is, in the gallery of your castle, a picture of Philippe de Champaigne, of exquisite finish, which pleases me beyond measure. Your Rubens are also to my taste, as well your smallest Watteau. In the salon to the right, I have noticed the Louis XIII cadence-table, the tapestries of Beauvais, the Empire gueridon signed 'Jacob,' and the Renaissance chest. In the salon to the left, all the cabinet full of jewels and miniatures.

For the present I will content myself with those articles that can be conveniently removed. I will therefore ask you to pack them carefully and ship them to me...within eight days, otherwise I shall be obliged to remove them myself during the night of 27 September; but, under those circumstances, I shall not content myself with the articles above mentioned....

Keep in mind that there is at this point no reason to believe that Lupin has ever been legitimately admitted into the baron's castle, despite which he seems to know where everything is, in the greatest detail. He has the audacity to inform the victim in advance of what precisely he intends to steal, and when, and is daring the authorities to stop him. The fun of these stories is the ingeniousness and panache with which he pulls off these crimes. He is, unsurprisingly, a master of disguise and appears under many aliases. In one story "Holmlock Shears Arrives Too Late," (later reprinted as "Sherlock Holmes Arrives too Late"), Lupin first matches wits with the great Sherlock Holmes. The contest is a draw. (He and Holmes would meet again.)

In "The Red Silk Scarf," Lupin delivers to his "friend," the much put-upon Ganimard, all the clues he needs to solve a murder and advance his career considerably, but Lupin also makes off with a valuable jewel, and so aids justice and plays the thief at the same time. In some of his later adventures, he began to be on the side of the law more often, but, as some commentators have noted, his heart doesn't seem to be in it.

Such "gentleman burglar" characters were not unique in late 19th or early 20th century crime fiction. The best known one in English is E.W. Hornung's "amateur cracksman" Raffles, whose adventures began in 1899. Leslie Charteris's much later creation, the Saint, is in the same tradition. Perhaps the thrill or fascination for audiences was the fact that these characters were *gentlemen*, i.e. persons of refinement and with (presumably) financial security, who don't *need* to embark on careers of crime, but do so as a game or sport, or even as an artform. The stories turn on *how* the crimes are carried out and often deal heavily in irony. The appeal is very similar to what Hollywood today calls a "caper film."

Leblanc tried to popularize other characters, such as private eye Jim Barnett, and even wrote two science fiction novels, but the public still demanded the immortal Lupin, and Leblanc spent most of the rest of his writing life producing them. The stories are still enormously entertaining, so it is clear to see why there was such demand. Leblanc was award a Legion of Honor for his services to French literature.

THE EYES OF INNOCENCE

THE EYES OF INNOCENCE

I

GILBERTE

"WOULD you please give your name, madam?" asked the waiter.

And he handed the elder of the two travellers a sheet of paper headed, *"Villa-pension des Deux Mondes, Dieppe."*

"Write down the name, Gilberte," she said. "I am so tired."

Gilberte took the pen and wrote:

"Mme. Armand and daughter, from London, bound for. . . . Now that I think of it, where are we going next, mother?"

"I don't know yet."

"Oh, that doesn't matter!" said the waiter.

And he took the paper and left the room.

"Yes, Mr. Waiter," cried the young girl, with a laugh. "Mme. Armand and her daughter, arriving from England, from Germany, from Russia, coming to France and delighted, especially Mlle. Armand, who does not yet know her own country!"

"Will you find happiness here?" murmured her mother, sadly, drawing her daughter to her. "There is none left for me, since your poor father is dead; but you, my pet, my dear, loving Gilberte, what has the future in store for you?"

"Why, joys, mother darling, nothing but the greatest joys: haven't I you with me?"

They exchanged a long embrace. Then Mme. Armand said:

"Gilberte, the crossing has upset me; I feel I must lie down for a while. Go and sit on the terrace and come back in an hour. Then we will unpack our trunks and go to the post-office."

"Are you expecting a letter?"

"Yes."

"From whom?"

"How inquisitive you are!"

"Oh, mummy, you're always saying that! But are you sure that it's not you who are a little—what shall I say—mysterious? You never answer even my simplest questions."

"I shall answer them one day, child, but not before I have to . . . not before I have to."

Gilberte saw her mother's face wrung with such anguish that she was silent and fondly kissed her hand. Mme. Armand went on:

"Yes, you are right. I am a little mysterious, very mysterious even; but if you only know how it hurts me to be so! Still, I will answer you this time, dear: the letter I am expecting is from your nurse."

"From my nurse? Then I was brought up in France? But where?"

Mme. Armand was silent. Gilberte waited a few moments, then put on her hat and cloak and said:

"Go and lie down, mother. You poor dear, you look as you do on your bad days. . . . There, I'll leave you in peace."

"You won't go out, will you, dear?"

"Go out? I, who have never left your side? Why, I should be afraid to walk down the street all by myself! I shall be back soon, dearest."

She opened the door and went downstairs. Above the reception-rooms, which occupied a wing consisting of a single floor, to the right of the garden, was a terrace covered with tents and wicker chairs. She sat down there.

It was a mild and balmy October day. The wide, deserted beach was bright with sunshine. The sea was very calm and edged with a narrow fringe of foam.

An hour passed.

"I will go in," she said, "when that little boat disappears behind the jetty."

The boat disappeared and she rose to her feet. As she went up the stairs, a childish idea came into her head, an idea which she was destined long to remember, together

with the smallest details of that terrible minute:

"If mother is still asleep," she thought, "I
will blow on her forehead to wake her."

She listened at the door. Not a sound.
She laughed roguishly. Then, slowly, cau-
tiously, she opened the door. Mme. Armand lay stretched on the bed. Gilberte
went up to her. For some indefinable reason, she forgot her intended joke and simply
kissed her mother on the forehead.

A cry escaped her lips. Terror-stricken,
she flung herself upon her mother, caught
her desperately in her arms and fell faint-
ing beside the bed.

Mme. Armand was dead.

* * *

A room in which she sobs for hours on end,
heedless of all things, huddled in a little
chair, or on her knees before a white-cur-
tained bed; people who come and go; a doctor who certifies the cause of death; aneurism
of the heart, beyond a doubt; the lady of the

house, who tries to comfort her; a commissary of police who puts questions which she
is unable to answer and who makes her look
in her mother's trunks for papers that are
not there: these are Gilberte's lasting memories of those two dreadful days.

Then came the singing in the church, a
long road between bare, wind-stripped trees,
the graveyard and the final and irrevocable
parting from her who, until now, was all her
life, her soul, her light. . . .

Oh, the first night spent in solitude and
those first meals taken with no one opposite
her and those long interminable days during
which she never stopped weeping the big
tears that come welling up from the heart
as from a spring which nothing can dry up!
Alone, knowing nobody, what was she to
do? Where could she go? To whom could
she turn?

"The important thing," insisted the lady
of the house, who sometimes came to see her
in her room, "the most important thing is

that you should have a solicitor. Mine is prepared to come whenever you please. I spoke to him about you; and it seems that there are formalities. Remember what the commissary said about the papers. . . ."

Gilberte remembered nothing, for she had listened to nothing. Nevertheless, the persistency of this advice, repeated daily and with such conviction, ended by persuading her; and, one morning, she sent to ask Maître Dufornéril to be good enough to call on her.

Maître Dufornéril had one of those placid and good-natured faces the sight of which seems to soothe you at once. He gave the impression of attaching so much importance to the business in hand that it would have been impossible not to take at least some interest in it one's self. Gilberte, therefore, was obliged to reflect, to tax her memory, in short, to reply.

"From what I have learnt, mademoiselle, it is evident that no papers have been found enabling us to establish your mother's identity and your own.   The commissary, however, told me of an envelope containing securities which he advised you to lock up carefully.   Is it still in your possession?"

"I don't know. . . . Mother never told me. . . . Is this what you mean?" she asked.

The solicitor took two fat, leather portfolios from the mantelpiece and opened them.   He was astounded at what he saw:

"And do you leave this lying about? . . . Bonds payable to bearer?"

Gilberte blushed, feeling as if she had committed some enormous crime.   He counted the sheets, made a rapid addition and said:

"You are very well off, mademoiselle."

"Really?" she said, absent-mindedly. "Yes . . . mother said something . . ."

After a peace during which he watched her with increasing surprise, he asked:

"And have you your mother's papers, your father's papers?"

"What papers?"

"Why, their birth-certificates, your own, their marriage-certificate, in fact, everything that established their position and now establishes yours."

"I haven't them."

"But they must be somewhere. . . . Can you give me no clue as to where they are?"

"No. . . . But I seem to remember once hearing them talk of papers that had been lost . . . or rather burnt in a fire . . . or else . . . in fact, I can't say for certain." . . .

"Come, come!" cried Maître Duforneril. "We are on the wrong track altogether! Let us start from the beginning. Where were you born?"

"I don't know."

"How do you mean, you don't know?"

"Mother would never tell me exactly."

"But where was she born? And your father?"

"I don't know that either."

The solicitor looked up. Was she laughing at him? But, at the sight of her sad face and candid eyes, he was silent for a moment and then went on:

"You have come from London?"

"Yes."

"Did you have friends over there, acquaintances?"

"No, we lived quite alone."

"Never mind: if you give me the address of the house you lived in, we shall easily find traces of Mme. Armand."

"Mother was not called Mme. Armand in London; she was called Aubert."

"But Armand is your real name?"

"I don't think so. At Liverpool, where we lived for three years and where father died, last year, after making such a lot of money, we were known by the name of Kill-

ner. Before that, at Berlin, it was Dumas.
. . . And, at Moscow" . . .

"You don't know the reason why your
parents used to change their name like
that?"

"No, I do not."

"You saw nothing in your parents' character to explain it?"

"No, nothing."

"Were they on good terms?"

"Oh, yes! They were so fond of each
other! And mother was so happy!"

So happy! How positively Gilberte was
able to say that! Happy indeed beside her
husband, under his eyes, with her hand in
his. But why was she so often caught crying? Why those hours of gloomy melancholy, of inexplicable depression? Why
had she one day drawn her daughter to her,
stammering:

"Ah, my child; my child! Never do anything that you have to hide: it is too painful!"

Gilberte was on the point of speaking. A vague sense of shame prevented her. Besides, Maître Dufornéril, who had taken down a few notes in his pocket-book, was beginning again:

"Give me all the particulars that can help us, mademoiselle.   The smallest details are of importance."

She mentioned the towns in which they had lived: Vienna, Trieste, Milan, with their memories of a secluded life, easy of late, but so hard and difficult at first; and then, further back, Barcelona, where they had been very unhappy; and then came memories, more and more indistinct, of poverty, hunger, cold. . . .

"We shall find out, mademoiselle," declared the solicitor.   "It won't be an easy business, for we have to do with a combination of abnormal circumstances which baffle me a little, I admit.   But, after all, it is inconceivable that we should not find out. You have to know, you must know who you are and what name you are entitled to bear. Will you trust your interests to me?"

"Yes."

"Well, first of all, you must leave this bundle of securities in my hands: I will give you a receipt for it. I will cash the coupons as they fall due and send you the proceeds when you need money. Where were you going with your mother?"

"She was expecting a letter."

"A letter? That is one clue."

"But the letter was addressed to the *póste restante;* and I don't know in what name or initials."

"True. . . Then what do you intend to do?"

"I intend to go somewhere at random. I have heard mother speak of Chartres, Saumer, Domfront. I shall choose one of those towns, the quietest . . . no matter where . . . as long as I can weep undisturbed."

"Poor child!" murmured Maître Dufornéril.

II

"OF the fortress built, in 1011, by Guillaume de Bellême, on the summit of the rock
at Domfront, at 300 feet above the little
River Varenne, all that is now left standing
is two great strips of wall, flanked by pictur-
esque buttresses and pierced with wide
arches, the remains of the ancient keep.
Round about are a few traces of ramparts
and remnants of underground passages, all
arranged in the form of a square and in a
perfect state of preservation."

The guide-books, however, for some reason, fail to mention the manor-house built,
in the seventeenth century, by Pierre de
Donnadieu, Governor of Anjou, on the site
and with the materials of the outbuildings
of the old fortress. The *logis,* as this sort of

dwelling is called in Lower Normandy, is intact and wholly charming. Four slender, tapering turrets grace the corners. An enormous roof, decked with two monumental chimneys, seems to top it with a fool's cap, too large for its little granite forehead lined with two rows of bricks. The entrance is through the square, but the main front overlooks the precipice and a garden staggers down the steep slope to the river that winds through the pretty Valdes Rochers.

Fourteen years earlier, M. and Mme. de la Vaudraye, one of the leading families of the neighborhood, had ruined themselves in unfortunate speculations. M. de la Vaudraye died of grief and shame. His widow, in order to pay for the education of her ten-year-old son, let the manor-house, which formed part of her dowry and which had been in the possession of her family for nearly two hundred years. It was taken, for a time, by one of the garrison officers, but was now once more untenanted.

Here Gilberte sought refuge like a poor wounded animal. The very sleepiness of Domfront had attracted her, its look as of some vanquished city, wearied of a valorous past and taking its just and honourable repose. Strolling through the ruins, she saw, on the door of the Logis, a notice, "To Let." She went in search of the owner.

Mme. de la Vaudraye, a tall, thin, hard-eyed woman, expressed herself in affected sentences of which her lips formed the syllables carefully, one by one, as though they were things of price that must be carried to the highest pitch of perfection.

"I can see from your attitude, madame," she said, "that you have been struck by the unimpeachable condition of my house. Woodwork, mirrors, curtains, furniture: everything is in perfect repair. And yet the Logis is one of the most historic abodes in the district" . . .

Gilberte was no longer listening. She

had been called, "Madame." It had seemed
natural then to address her like that? If
so, could she pass as married, in spite of her
age? The thought surprised her. And
yet, she reflected, how could any one suppose
that a young girl would come by herself to
treat for the manor-house and live in it by
herself?

She remembered a piece of advice which
the solicitor had given her:

"If you wish to lead a quiet life, not a
word about the past before we have shed a
full light upon it."

Yes, but how much easier it would be to
veil the past under that name of "madame"!
And how much better that title would protect her! As a girl, living alone, she must
needs be the object of curiosity, the victim of
any amount of gossip. As a married woman,
she would be in a normal position; her
solitary existence would cause no surprise;
she could keep off intruders, go about as
she pleased, or stay indoors and weep, with

none to spy upon the secret of her tears.

"In what name shall I make out the agreement?" asked Mme. de la Vaudraye, when everything was settled: settled to the great advantage of the owner, who had increased her rent by one-half.

"Why, in my own name: Mme. Armand!" said Gilberte, without foreseeing the consequences which this decision involved.

Mme. de la Vaudraye hesitated:

"But . . . perhaps we shall want . . . M. Armand's signature" . . .

"I am a widow."

"Oh, I beg your pardon!   I ought to have known.   I see you are in mourning" . . .

Mme. Armand moved into the Logis that same evening.   At Mme. de la Vaudraye's express recommendation, she engaged as a servant the wife of the keeper of the ruins, Adèle, a big, fat, talkative woman, with hair on her upper lip, a stealthy eye and quick, blunt manners.   Bouquetot, her husband, was to sleep at the manor-house; and their son, Antoine, who had just left his regiment, would do the heavy work and attend to the garden.

* * *

And life began, the hard, cruel, despairing life of those who have no one to love them and no one whom they can love.

There was no consolation for Gilberte, after her mother's death. What saved her was the necessity to act, to act continually, to make decisions, to give orders, in short, to exercise her will. She had to shake off her natural inclination for dreaming and listlessness, to break herself of the passive habits due to the existence which she had led till then. Things went so badly at the manorhouse until she realized the task that lay before her, the domestic duties were so irregularly performed, there was so much fuss and disorder, that she was compelled to look after her own housekeeping.

She found it difficult indeed to word the first reprimand:

"Adèle, I do wish you would serve lunch punctually!"

And she added, immediately:

"Of course, I mean, when possible."

As ill-luck would have it, it was not "possible" for three days running; and Gilberte had to resolve to speak seriously. On the fourth day, she went down to the kitchen, very quickly, so as not to let her indignation cool on the stairs:

"Adèle! It's one o'clock and" . . .

"Well, what of it?" the fat woman broke in.

Gilberte stopped short, hesitated, blushed and stammered:

"I should so much like to have luncheon served at half-past twelve exactly!"

From that day forward, the meals were punctually prepared.

Her victory gave her self-assurance. She had the accounts brought to her daily, although her inspection was confined to ascertaining the cost of things and checking the additions.

With Gilberte's affection and open nature, however, it was difficult for her to live absolutely cut off from her fellow-creatures, as she had first intended. True, she refused to make acquaintances; and her shyness was such that, after three months, she had not yet set foot in the streets of Domfront. But those who have been stricken by fate have a natural company of friends in the poor, the wretched, the destitute, the outcast; and her heart could not avoid the sort of friendship built upon adversity.

Between Gilberte and the first beggar who crossed the threshold of the Logis there was more than an alms and a thank-you: there was the delight of giving on one side and, on the other, gratitude for the smile and the good grace of her who gave. Nor could it be otherwise. Even if Gilberte had not had that pretty, fair hair which frolicked

around her face like little flickering flames,
nor those gentle lips, nor those pink cheeks
which gave her face the freshness of a flower,
she would still have been bewitchingly beautiful, thanks to her blue eyes, which were
always a little dewy, as though tears were
playing in them, and always smiling, even at
the times of her deepest sadness. And her
look, her figure, all her delicate and attractive personality breathed such touching purity that the most indifferent were lapped in
it as in the soft caresses of a balmy breeze.

Her charm was made up of goodness, simplicity and, above all, innocence, that innocence which is unaware of its own existence,
which knows nothing of life, which suspects
no evil and which does not see the traps laid
for it, nor the hypocrisy that surrounds it,
nor the envy which it inspires.

La Bonne Demoiselle was the name by
which the poor called her, thus correcting,
by a sort of common instinct, the style which
circumstances had compelled her to adopt.

And, in all the garrets of Domfront, in all
the cabins and cottages of the neighbourhood,
people spoke of *la Bonne Demoiselle* of the
Logis, of *la Bonne Demoiselle* who mourned
her husband's memory and smiled upon the
poor.

Her gentle smile worked many a miracle
in that little world, dispelled many a hatred,
stifled many a rebellious impulse, healed
many a sore.   Men and women consulted
her, inexperienced girl that she was, and,
what was more, followed her advice.

A mother came one day, with her baby in
her arms.   She told the tragedy of her life,
spoke of an elopement, a desertion.   Gilberte understood nothing of her story.   Yet
the mother, in an hour, went away consoled.

Young girls came and asked her opinion
about getting married; women came and
enlarged upon their domestic quarrels;
others came and told her things that bewildered her.   All these problems, all these
cases of conscience Mme. Armand, *la Bonne*

Demoiselle, solved with her innocence, the innocence of a child that, knowing nothing, knows more than they who know everything.

One evening, Adèle brought her house-keeping-book. Gilberte gravely added the column and initialed it.

"But madame is not even looking to see what I bought and how much I paid."

Gilberte blushed:

"You see. . . . I don't know much about it. . . . So I leave it to you. . . . Besides, I have no reason to suspect you. . . ."

There must have been something in the tone of her words, something special in her air and attitude; at any rate, the old woman was seized with extraordinary excitement, and, flinging herself on her knees before her mistress, cried:

"Oh, it's a shame to cheat a person like you, ma'am! I can have no heart at all, nor my great rascal of a Bouquetot either! . . . Why, you must be an angel from Heaven not to see that everybody's robbing you: the

grocer, the baker, the butcher, and I most
of all! . . . Just look at my book: a bunch
of carrots, thirty sous; a wretched chicken,
six francs fifteen sous. . . ."

She emptied her purse on the table:

"There! Fifty or sixty francs I've done
you out of, all in one month! . . . But I
stopped the other day, I couldn't do it, it
broke my heart to see you like that, so trust-
ing. . . ."

"My poor Adèle," whispered Gilberte,
greatly moved.

"And then . . . and then," continued the
woman, in a low voice, with bent head, "I
have something else to confess. . . . But I
dare not: it's so shameful. . . . Listen. . . .
Mme. de la Vaudraye . . . well, she put me
here to tell her all about you: what you did;
if you received any letters; if you talked to
gentlemen. . . . And, in the morning, when
I went to do my shopping, I used to go to
her . . . and tell her what I saw. . . . Oh,
there was nothing wrong to tell, for you are

a real saint! . . . But, all the same. . . . Forgive me!"

The old servant's confusion was touching. Gilberte gently raised her from the floor and said:

"There, we'll say no more about it. But why is Mme. de la Vaudraye interested in me and my doings?"

"Goodness knows! She's always poking her nose in everywhere and wants to manage everything at Domfront and every one to obey her. And you don't know how they talk about you here! There's no lack of gossip, I can tell you!"

"About me?"

"Yes. They want to know where you come from, who M. Armand was, all sorts of things! Then Mme. de la Vaudraye speechifies about you in her drawing-room. Just think, you're her tenant; and she's the only one who has spoken to you! . . . And then I've guessed something else. . . ."

"What's that, Adèle?"

"Well, you are rich and a widow; I'm sure she's after you as a daughter-in-law. . . . That I'd take my oath on! . . . Oh, she has her head screwed on her shoulders! A fine lady like you for her penniless beggar of a son, a good-for-nothing who can't put his hand to anything! . . ."

Gilberte listened to her in utter confusion. Wasn't it possible to remain hidden and unknown? Were there really people who spied on others, who tried to fathom the mystery of their lives and actually plotted against them?

But Adèle said, in a big, fond voice:

"Don't you worry yourself, *ma Bonne Demoiselle*. I'm here and I'll look after you and look after your money. Oh, the grocer and the butcher and the rest had best mind what they're about! . . . You let me be: you won't be overcharged any more. . . . And then Bouquetot is there and my son Antoine: they're decent fellows both . . . and fell in love with you at once . . .

because . . . because there's something different about you . . . something that makes
people love you . . . in spite of themselves
. . . with all their hearts. . . ."

III

EVERY day, when her household duties were done, Gilberte walked in her garden. This was her hour of recreation. But a sweeter hour followed, which she allotted to dreaming.

High up, on the left, on a jutting promontory, was a clearing where stood the ruins of a little summer-house. The view from here extended, over undulating plains, to the dark heights of Mortain. On the right, the other side of the valley was a wall of red rocks, clad in broom and fir-trees. It was a landscape of illimitable distances and, at the same time, tender and familiar through the homeliness of this little glen, a landscape which had all the wild and rugged poetry of a Breton moor. . . .

The daylight waned early in those winter

months. Gilberte waited until the veil of
night smothered its last glimmers. Sometimes, the sun's reflections would linger on
the motionless clouds. Then the darkness
seemed to come from every side, to rise from
the river, to fall from the overcast sky, to
ooze from the earth in thick mists. Then
Gilberte would go indoors.

But, one evening, at that murky moment
of twilight, she saw, on the opposite slope, a
human form issuing from a hollow among
the rocks and vanishing behind a tree.

She would hardly have paid attention to
it, if, on the next day, when her eyes turned
in that direction on returning from her
walk, she had not perceived, in the same
place, the same form as on the day before:
a man's figure, obviously, but so well hidden
that it was impossible for her to distinguish
the least detail of his face or dress.

On the day after that, he was not there;
but he was there on the following day and
almost every day afterwards.

Gilberte soon noticed that he slipped through the fir-trees a little before her arrival and went away soon after she was gone.

Then was he there for her? She did not ask herself this question, but, all unwittingly, she was pleased at the fact that some one was there, dreaming doubtless like herself, some one whom she did not know, who was not seeking to know her and of whom she thought only as an invisible companion, a more or less real ghost, a freak of her imagination. She had not the least curiosity concerning others and would never have supposed that any one could have the least curiosity concerning her. He was there for the same reasons that brought her there, because it is good to see night blend with day and because that twilight hour is full of charm and peace.

And so she had a friend, a distant and inaccessible friend, from whom she would have hidden herself for ever, if he had dared to show himself or even let her see by a move-

ment that he was there for her, but who did
not frighten her, for the sole reason that he
seemed to have no actual existence.

"Are you not afraid of catching cold, dear
madame?"

It was Mme. de la Vaudraye, who took
her by surprise one evening, at the summer-
house and at once continued, in her affected
voice:

"I owe you a thousand apologies. The
merest politeness demanded that I should
pay you a visit, but what shall I say? I
have so many duties, so many cares! I am
the president of a number of charitable com-
mittees which take up all my time. Besides,
I confess, I was afraid of appearing indis-
creet. I so much dread to push myself forward! Still, I thought it was time to try
and bring some diversion into the nun's life
which you are leading."

"You are too kind," said Gilberte, touched
by this solicitude.

"I felt, dear madame, that your days must

be so dull. Your evenings especially must
seem endless. How do you manage to fill
them?"

They had returned to the Logis. A good
fire warmed the boudoir in which Gilberte
liked best to sit. The lamp was lighted.
There was some music on the piano. The
table was heaped with books and papers.

"You see, madame, I play and read: I
read a great deal."

"Novels, I expect!" said the visitor, with
a titter. "May I look? . . . What have we
here? An atlas . . . manuals of history
. . . and literature . . . selected essays . . .
memoirs! Are you superintending somebody's education?"

"My own," said Gilberte, laughing. "It
has been a little neglected; and, as I have
plenty of time . . ."

"But many of the books are in English
. . . in German even . . ."

"I know English and German."

"Quite a learned person! But how well

you would get on with my son! He is so studious and cultured! He writes for the Paris papers. . . . Not under his own name, of course: he would never consent to commit the name of La Vaudraye to an occupation which, after all, is only an amusement. He quite agrees with me on that question . . . as on every other. . . . Why don't you come to us one evening? We have a few friends who are pleased to make my drawing-room their daily meeting-place. . . . Everybody is dying to see you, Guillaume most of all. . . ."

His mother's description of young Guillaume de la Vaudraye was hardly of a nature to charm Gilberte from her isolation. She found an excuse.

"You are making a mistake," cried Mme. de la Vaudraye, who was irritated by her refusal. "Good friends are a necessity: they protect you against evil tongues."

"Evil tongues?"

"Yes, yes, you can understand that one

can't live as you do without attracting comment in a small town. People ask themselves—and not without some justice, as you must admit—the reason of your voluntary imprisonment. All the more so because, as I hear, your servant, Adèle, keeps a silent tongue in her head; and that sets public opinion against you. Lastly, they say . . ."

"What?"

"Well, they say that you are leading such a secret existence because . . ."

"Because what?"

Mme. de la Vaudraye hesitated, or rather seemed to hesitate, and then blurted out:

"Because you do not live alone."

She rose, thinking that Gilberte must be crushed under this accusation. But Gilberte, casting about ingenuously for what her visitor could have meant, repeated:

"Not alone! Well, of course not, as Adèle is here, with her husband and her son!"

"There, don't be alarmed, child," con-

cluded Mme. de la Vaudraye, in a patroniz-
ing little way. "That is only so much talk
and gossip, which I shall know how to put
down, if you will help me. It only wants a
small sacrifice. For instance, I shall be
making the collection at High Mass, on Sunday: promise me to come. It's a promise,
isn't it?" she said, as she went away.

Gilberte would much rather have stayed
quietly at home; but, as she had been told
that that was impossible, she gave up the
idea:

"It seems to hurt people," she said to herself.

And, on the Sunday morning, when the
bells rang for mass, she left the Logis for
the first time.

She felt, in the crowded high-street, as
though she were awaking from a dream of
peace and silence, so intense was her dislike
of bustle and noise. There were people at
the windows, people at the shop-doors, people in the church-porch; and all those people

were watching her, staring at her and whispering as she passed.

The church was a refuge, despite the crowd that filled it and despite the excitement provoked by her presence. Every one was astounded at her youthfulness, dazzled by her beauty. When she walked down the nave again, a murmur of admiration rippled through the rows of worshippers. But, when she reached the holy-water basin, an incident occurred that delayed her for a few seconds. Three men had rushed forward. And, with one movement, three hands were dipped into the marble basin and held out to her. She lowered her veil and went on.

Outside the church, the crowd stood waiting for her. Gilberte hurried along, feeling her shyness returning in the sunlight. Her one idea was to get back to the Logis, back into the shade. But there was a pastry-cook's shop at the end of the high-street; she caught sight of the window crammed

with dainty custards and many-coloured
cakes; and, as she was not prepared for such
a temptation, she succumbed.

Slowly and hesitatingly, she made her
choice.   The shop-woman did up the parcel;
Gilberte took it and moved away.   But at
the door she stopped, timidly.   A group of
street-boys was standing outside.

There they were, with their hands in their
pockets, like loafers feasting their eyes on an
unusual sight.   She went out.   They ran on
either side of her, making a great din with
their wooden shoes.   Gilberte suffered tor-
tures.

Suddenly, she heard cries and laughter
behind her.   She turned round.   A young
man, whom she recognized as one of the
three who offered her the holy water, had
darted into the midst of her escort and was
dispersing it with uplifted cane.   She bowed
her head, in sign of thanks, and continued on
her way.

An hour later, as she was finishing lunch,

Adèle brought her an enormous sheaf of flowers: roses, white lilac and camellias. A peasant had handed them to the servant without a word of explanation.

"But I know who sent them," said Adèle. "It can only be M. Beaufrelant. He has the finest hot-houses in the district; he is mad on flowers. Madame must have seen him in church: a tall, thin man, with whiskers."

Bouquetot, Adèle's husband, entered:

"An old woman has brought this letter for madame."

Gilberte opened the envelope. It contained a thousand-franc note and a few words written in a copper-plate hand on pink note-paper:

"To Mme. Armand, for her poor."

"A bank-note! It must be that money-bags of a M. le Hourteulx. Let me see the hand-writing. . . . Yes, that's right; I was in service with him. . . . Oh, my fine fellow, if you think that, because you possess hun-

dreds and thousands! . . . Not a word. . . .
I know what's what!"

Bouquetot said to his wife: ,

"I met Mme. Duval, the chair-attendant,
in the town just now. She told me that M.
Beaufrelant and M. le Hourteulx were
standing by the holy-water basin in church
this morning; and young Simare as well.
And then the barber told me that young Simare followed madame and drove away the
street-boys who ran after her."

Gilberte thought for a moment and said:

"Go to Mme. de la Vaudraye, Adèle, tell
her how this money and these flowers came
into my hands and ask her to oblige me by
returning them to the senders. But the
poor must not be the losers; and here is another thousand-franc note which I beg that
she will distribute as she thinks best."

That afternoon, Gilberte remained pen-
sive. Those two presents surprised her.
Her ignorance of social usages did not allow
her to see any indelicacy or indiscretion in

the way in which they were offered; and yet she felt that there was something that should not have been done.

"What does it mean?" she wondered, with a vague anxiety. "What do they want with me?"

It was the outside world trying to insinuate itself into her peaceful home, into her independent life: the world with its sordid calculations, its intrigues, its vanities, its stealthy encroachments upon those who seek solitude, its instinctive jealousy of those who are able to do without it.

At nightfall, she walked to the ruined summer-house. The stranger was there, among the rocks opposite. She recovered all her serenity. And not for a second did the idea cross her mind that he might be one of the three who had forced their attentions upon her.

IV

AN EVENING AT MME. DE LA VAUDRAYE'S

IT would be wearisome to describe the
long series of moves and machinations, the
whole comedy of affectation and pretended
solicitude which Mme. de la Vaudraye employed to induce Gilberte to come and see
her. One day, at last, Gilberte promised,
on the understanding that there would be no
one there but the regular visitors to the
house.

And, in the evening, Adèle, carrying a
lantern and muttering between her teeth,
accompanied her through the deserted
streets.

It was a very modest house that was occu-
pied by her who remained the first lady of
Domfront despite her shattered fortunes.
No show, no comfort, hardly room for the

mother and son; but there was a *salon,* a
sumptuous *salon,* a *salon,* to which everything had been sacrificed, a *salon* that en-
abled Mme. de la Vaudraye to declare, with
pride:

"I have a *salon.*"

And the townspeople nodded their heads
in chorus:

"Mme. de la Vaudraye has a *salon.*"

In so saying, they had in mind not only
the costly furniture heaped up in that one
room, but also the shining lights of the town
who adorned it with their presence. You
were really nobody at Domfront if you did
not form part of the *salon* of Mme. de la
Vaudraye.

In its essence and as Gilberte saw it, the
salon consisted of an old-oak chest and an
Empire sideboard, of the Bottentuit and
Charmeron couples and their five young
ladies, of M. and Mme. Lartiste and their
son, of Mlle. du Bocage, of M. Beaufrelant,
M. Hourteulx and Messrs. Simare, father

and son, of a Louis XV clock, of a lacquered glass-case, and of a set of chairs and arm-chairs upholstered in crimson silk.

A great silence, composed of eager curiosity, admiration and envy, greeted Gilberte's entrance. The hostess at once made the introductions, or rather chiselled them out in elaborate phrases. Gilberte bowed.

"And my son? Where is my dear Guillaume?"

He was extracted from a small side-room.

"Dear Mme. Armand, here is my Guillaume, who is so anxious to make your acquaintance."

Guillaume de la Vaudraye was not at all bad-looking, with a very good figure; but he had a sullen expression and his manners seemed constrained. He gave a bow and vanished.

There was an attempt at general conversation, which fell very flat. People exchanged distressful looks and dared not raise their voices. Gilberte did not utter a word.

Then, to break the ice, a rush was made
for the principal person present, the last re-
source of drawing-rooms. He always lords
it in the place of honour, displaying the ex-
pansive smile of his large yellow teeth. He
looks like a squatting Hindu idol; he is well-
groomed, shiny and pretentious. He is the
centre of social life, the ever-ready rescuer,
the life and soul of the company, the master
of ceremonies, the master of the revels, the
vanisher of intolerable silence. And none
can contest his supremacy, for he alone is
capable of making so much noise without becoming exhausted and of making more noise
by himself than all the rest put together.
The specimen in Mme. de la Vaudraye's
drawing-room was signed, "Pleyel."

It was as though the parts had been
allotted beforehand. Two groups were
formed: the audience and the performers.
Gilberte found herself seated between Mme.
Charmeron, who was famed for her persist-
ent dumbness and distinction, and M. Simare

junior, the best-dressed and most dissipated young man in the town. He went twice a year to Paris and was looked upon as a master of wit and satire. As a matter of fact, he started chaffing at once:

"Ah, the overture of *The Bronze Horse* by a Demoiselle Charmeron and a Demoiselle Bottentuit! That's the invariable first piece here. Ten years ago, it seems, it was played by Mme. Bottentuit and her sister, Mme. Charmeron; to-day, their heiresses are following in their footsteps. Observe how beautifully the two young ladies hold themselves. Their ambition is to realize the back view of a pair of sticks. They practise it for four hours every morning. . . ."

When the last chords had been banged out, he continued:

"Now, the little Charmeron girl will move off on the right, taking her stool with her, and the little Bottentuit girl will slide to the middle of the key-board. From the performer that she was she will become the ac-

companist of papa. There, what did I tell
you? It's all settled beforehand! Look
out! Maître Bottentuit, the attorney, the
drawing-room howler, is going off, going off,
I say. . . . I defy you to make out a word
he sings. . . . People have been trying for
ten years; and no one has ever succeeded.
. . . Excuse me . . . got to stop . . . can't
hear myself talk . . . the wretch is bawling
too loud. . . ."

After Maître Bottentuit, Mlle. du Bocage
—a little old maid whose mouth opened so
wide that you could have dived down her
throat—struck up the duet in *Mireille,* sup-
ported by M. Lartiste the elder, an old man,
with a clean-shaven face, whose mouth, on
the contrary, remained hermetically closed,
with the résults that both parts of the duet—
not only the cooing roulades of the woman,
but also the frenzied appeals of the man, his
prayers, his promises, his metamorphoses
into a bird and a butterfly—seemed to issue
from the yawning throat of Mireille, that

gulf where you saw a host of little pieces of mechanism madly at work. The loving couple had a great success.

"M. le Hourteulx next," said young Simare. "Our millionaire is going to sing for you, madame, for, you know, he has been smitten with a passion since he saw you in church; a passion shared, of course, by his enemy Beaufrelant, for the two men always form the same wishes, so as to have the pleasure of thwarting each other. It's a long-standing hatred: le Hourteulx was married once; and it seems that Beaufrelant . . ."

Simare bent over towards Gilberte and whispered a few words in her ear.

Young Lartiste, who owed his fame as a great actor to his name and to his name alone, was reserved for the end.

"No one recites like young Lartiste," people said at Domfront.

And, from the first words that he spoke, everybody watched Gilberte, to enjoy her amazement. Unfortunately, Simare was

continuing his more or less decorous reflexions; and Gilberte, although not always
catching his exact meaning, felt so uncom-
fortable that she did not listen to young Lartiste at all and forgot to applaud at the
striking passages, an omission that was put
down to her bad taste.

"Mme. de la Vaudraye is furious," said
Simare. "Her son's gone. And I expect
she jolly well lectured him about making
himself agreeable to you. By Jove, when
you're a mother, you have to think of your
son's future. But Guillaume making himself agreeable is a sight that was never yet
seen! Besides, he looks down upon us too
much to remain in the drawing-room. Just
fancy, a writer like him! . . . Oh, I say, madame, look at the eyes Beaufrelant's making
at you! Beaufrelant is the Don Juan of
Domfront. No one can resist him. They
even say . . . but I don't know if I ought.
. . . Pooh, you have a fan . . . if you want
to blush. . . ."

And he again leant over towards Gilberte.

She rose from her seat at the first words. Mme. de la Vaudraye came running up to her:

"I am sure that that scapegrace of a Simare is saying all sorts of things that he shouldn't."

She drew her aside:

"Be careful with him, my child," she said. "I can see through his designs: he is trying to compromise you.   He is head over ears in debt and hunting for a fortune. . . . But haven't you seen Guillaume?   Wait for me here, I'll bring him to you."

Simare came up to Gilberte:

"I must apologize to you, madame; I shocked you just now."

"No, no," stammered Gilberte, driven to her wits' end by this persistency, "only I thought I ought not to . . ."

He interrupted her:

"It was I who ought not.   I couldn't help it: I was talking, talking a little at random, lest I should say what I have no right to say, what lies deep down within myself, one of those involuntary sentiments. . . ."

"I am so sorry, Mme. Armand," cried the hostess, returning. "My son was a little tired and has gone up to his room."

The musical and literary evening was over. But the resources of the la Vaudraye *salon* did not end there. Its frequenters prided themselves on knowing how to talk. And the conversation went by rule, of course, as everything went by rule in this society which, by the almost daily repetition of the same acts, had established habits as strong as immutable laws.

The licensed talkers were M. Beaufrelant, who, they said, cultivated the flowers of rhetoric with the same zeal and the same success as the flowers of the soil; Mme. de la Vaudraye, who specialized in literary discussions; M. Lartiste, who, as a printer, was naturally marked out for the loftiest philosophical speculations; M. Simare the elder,

a remarkable spinner of anecdotes; and,
lastly, M. Charmeron and his sister-in-law,
Mme. Bottentuit, who found, in their morbid
need for contradicting and disputing with
each other, an inexhaustible source of opin-
ions, witticisms and banter.   Outside these
privileged and, so to speak, official protago-
nists, it was very seldom that any one ventured to open his mouth.

Gilberte, who was beginning to feel terribly bored, listened without a word, which
was taken for a sign of admiring deference.
The truth is that this oratorical joust surprised her greatly.   All these people, speaking turn and turn about, seemed to be pur-
suing so many different conversations, each
of them thinking only of shining in the de-
partment that had devolved upon himself.
M. Lartiste, who had talked his best on capital punishment, the subject in which he ex-
celled, was answered by Mme. de la Vaudraye with a vigorous parallel between the
respective merits of Victor Hugo and La-

martine, which parallel was duly refuted in
a lyrical outburst from M. Beaufrelant on
the bulbs of the double dahlia.

And the utmost seriousness presided over
all this incoherence, each disputant con-
founding, with deadly earnestness, the inter-
locutor in whom he saw such another indom-
itable as himself. And the dumb circle of
hearers listened with nods and grunts of approval, as though these strange discussions
had excited them to the highest pitch.

"Well . . . and you?" said Mme. de la
Vaudraye to M. Simare the elder, at the
exact moment when the ardour of the tour-
ney seemed about to wane. "Are you not in
form to-day?"

M. Simare, the anecdotist, smiled. His
strong point lay in saying nothing until he
was questioned; and his dry silence, rich in
promise, lent enormous value to the one an-
ecdote to which he treated you each evening,
after carefully preparing, polishing, repol-
ishing and chipping it like a precious stone.

Everybody burst out laughing before he
even opened his mouth: it was understood
from his manner that the story would be a
little . . . naughty.

He said:

"I do not know if I can speak.   There are
young ears present."

A movement on the part of the mothers,
a glance; and the five young ladies disappeared "without seeming to."

He insisted:

"All the same, I feel bound to warn you
that it is a very risqué story.   I shall call
a spade a spade: local colour demands
it."

"Go on, M. Simare!" said somebody.
"We are all married people here!"

Gilberte was sitting in the front row of
chairs, understanding nothing of the departure of the young girls nor of all this pream-
able and in absolute ignorance of what was
looming ahead.

M. Simare walked up to her, bowed to her

gallantly, like a bull-fighter dedicating his next feat of prowess to the most prominent person present and sat down four feet in front of her.   And he began:

"The setting first, madame.   Picture the skirt of a wood: *dramatis personœ,* Fanchon and her friend Colin, who is whispering sweet nothings in her ear, very much in her ear, and . . . but wait!   At no great distance, in the middle of the wood, his reverence the rector is strolling, reading his breviary; and his walk takes him in the direction of our young rustics. . . . He comes. . . . He comes nearer and nearer. . . . Do you see the picture, madame?"

"Yes, yes," said Gilberte, earnestly, like a child who is interested in a fairy-tale. "What next?"

"The sun darts his rays through the branches, from the patches of blue sky. . . ."

He continued his description at length, talked of the rector and the birds and the flowers and the cool shade of the trees; and, strange to say, there was not another word about Fanchon and Colin.

"M. Simare is a little discursive this evening," whispered somebody. "He is not coming to the point as quickly as usual."

In fact, he was veering away from it, with his eyes fixed on Gilberte, who listened eagerly and who repeated, at intervals:

"And then? What next?"

Thereupon, he got more and more entangled in the poetic stroll of the rector, who kept on walking and never seemed to come as far as Fanchon and Colin. And it was Gilberte who, at last, exclaimed:

"But what became of Colin and Fanchon?"

Then the old boy made a decisive gesture:

"I can't, I can't tell you. . . . No, I won't tell you. . . ."

Everybody rose. Everybody protested.

M. Simare took refuge in laughter:

"Well, no, I won't tell you."

"But why not?"

"Why not? I don't know! It's her eyes.
. . . There are words one can't utter when
one looks at her, there are things one can't
tell."

He was no longer laughing. The others
were silent. And he continued:

"Look at her eyes. They gaze at you so
softly, so innocently. . . . All the time that
I was talking my nonsense, I wanted to in-
vent something for her, something about
saints and angels and a good little girl who
loves her mother and only thinks of pleas-
ing her and is happy from morning till
night. . . ."

V

THE SUITORS

GILBERTE went to more of Mme. de la Vaudraye's evenings: not that she liked them much; but she did not wish to have it thought that she disliked them.

And her presence delighted all the frequenters of the *salon,* the most cross-grained ladies and the most indifferent men alike. It was a curious influence exercised by that mere child; and she owed it neither to her experience—for what did she know of life?—nor to her tact—for what aim had she in view?—but to an inexplicable charm which affected all who came near her and which, at the same time, protected her against them. Her innocence was a greater attraction than any subtlety or intellectual charm and defended her to better purpose than prudence would have done or cleverness.

Old Simare was mad about her. Mme. Bottentuit told her all the secrets of her home life. Mme. Charmeron confided to her that she was broken-hearted at having nothing but daughters, but that she had not given up hope yet. Mlle. du Bocage hid her head on Gilberte's shoulder, wept and told her all her old-maidenly disappointments and regrets.

"You are the ornament of my *salon,* Gilberte," said Mme. de la Vaudraye.

She was not jealous of her. Gilberte, with her exquisite compassion, had guessed that the former lady of the Logis must still suffer from the ruin of her fortunes, must still feel how stunted and narrow was her life; and she showed her more attention than she did to any other.

Out of kindness to the mother she even tried to win the son's sympathies; but here she encountered a medley of such shyness

and rudeness, so unlovable a nature and so
marked a determination to repel her ad-
vances and treat her as he treated the other
frequenters of the *salon* that Gilberte was
quite discomfited.

"Do not be discouraged," said the mother.
"He is a little unsociable; but he is so full of
good qualities."

Nevertheless, Gilberte once heard her
mutter between her teeth:

"What a bear that boy is!"

And she heard on all sides that mother and
son did not agree.

The *salon* underwent a change. There
were as many commonplaces uttered as ever;
but those who spoke them did so with less
smug importance than before. People were
less sure of themselves. The talented ama-
teurs in singing and piano-playing sought
for shades of expression and feeling.
Lastly, the order of the concert became "subject to alterations" and the performers no
longer wore the air of automata obeying pre-

destined laws. There were asides in the
conversation; people talked among themselves, for the pleasure of talking and in
accordance with their various sympathies.

One evening, Beaufrelant drew Gilberte
into a corner and said:

"I am mad, madame, do you hear? I am
mad. I care for nothing, I am indifferent
to my flowers, it is you all the time. I am
free: my name, my life are yours; give me
some hope. . . ."

The next day, le Hourteulx made his declaration:

"Life has become a burden to me. If you
do not take pity on me, madame, I shall
cease to exist. . . . But I can hardly believe
that you will reject me. . . . Do you dislike me? . . . I am a widower and well-off,
you know. . . ."

That was the only dark spot that troubled
Gilberte's serenity: the more or less discreet
attentions which all those men paid her. Simare the younger went far more cleverly to

work and tried to inspire confidence with a pretence of delicacy by which Gilberte allowed herself to be taken in. But Beaufrelant and Le Hourteulx showed no pity: they pursued her relentlessly, speaking to her, not unnaturally, as to a woman who knows what life is and who could not well take offence at a declaration or even at the terms in which it was made.

Poor Gilberte did not take offence, but she was very much surprised; and the sighs and transports of those two men of forty bored her terribly. She avoided them and she also had to avoid young Lartiste, who tried the effect of poetry and fired the most passionate verses of Musset and Verlaine at her; the brother too of the Demoiselles Bottentuit, a schoolboy who was only let out on Thursdays and Sundays and who, the third time he saw her, threatened to kill himself at her feet; and lastly a cousin of Mlle. du Bocage, who was engaged to the elder Charmeron girl and who offered to break off the marriage and abandon a very good match if it caused her the faintest annoyance.

She no longer enjoyed at the Logis the atmosphere of peace and isolation so dear to her. Adèle had to defend the door, with the vigilance of a watch-dog, against the daring suitors who tried to obtain admission to her mistress upon some pretext:

"Madame is at home to nobody; I have positive instructions."

The old servant saw through the disguise of M. le Hourteulx, who appeared dressed up as a beggar, and of Beaufrelant, who, in cap and blouse, came round with a green-grocer's barrow.

Gilberte could not go for a stroll in her garden without seeing the figure of one or other of those importunate gentlemen on the right, in the next garden which ran from the castle down to the river. At nightfall, she was conscious of shadowy forms prowling

round the manor-house. She felt herself
spied upon on every side, stalked like a beast
of the chase.

It was Easter Sunday. After dinner,
Adèle and her husband went to the fair, just
outside the town. Gilberte was left alone.

It had been raining; and the fresh smell of
wet leaves and moist earth came through the
open window of the boudoir which she had
made into her study. The book which she
was reading in an absent-minded way
dropped to her lap and she sat dreaming,
with her gaze lost in the blackness of the
trees. And, quite without reason—for the
least sound would have struck her ear—she
was overcome with an indescribable sense of
dread, which increased from moment to moment. The silence seemed to her unnatural
and awful. The darkness was heavy with
menace; and she could not take her eyes
from it, sat spellbound by the unknown peril
which she felt was there.

A recollection doubled her fears. On the evening before at Mme. de la Vaudraye's, a turn in the conversation had led her to say that her servants were going to this fair. So they knew that she was all alone at the Logis.

Her one thought was to close the window, fasten down the shutters and place an obstacle between herself and the snares that were being laid for her in the threatening darkness; and yet she dared not stir, as though the least movement would have exposed her to immediate dangers. . . . But what dangers?

She made an effort and rose from her chair. At the same moment, a head appeared and a man strode across the balcony and sprang into the room. It was Simare.

The revulsion of feeling was such that she almost felt inclined to laugh. Wearily, she sat down and murmured:

"Oh, monsieur, you ought not to have done this! . . . I should never have thought it of you. . . ."

He flung himself on his knees:

"Do not judge me unheard. . . . I am not master of myself. . . . I have to go away for a month . . . and I wanted to see you . . . to tell you what I feel, what I suffer. . . . Oh, you don't know how your indifference has tortured me. . . . My sadness, my admiration, my hopes, my emotion, when in your presence: you have understood none of these . . . but then you never do understand. . . . At this very moment, when I am here, at your knees, when I am imploring you, when I am proclaiming my sorrow and my obsession, I feel that my words do not reach you. And yet they must. You must, you shall know what I have to say to you. . . . Listen to me. . . ."

But Gilberte would not listen. Although her extreme innocence had preserved her at first contact with the world, nevertheless she was beginning to see a glimmer of the meaning of many things; and she was frightened of the words that were coming. No, she would not hear them from the lips of this man, she would not allow this man to be the first to speak them in her ear. She had a sudden intuition of their importance and their sweetness and their magic; and she felt that it was almost a contamination to hear them.

She entreated him:

"Be quiet. . . . I shall be so grateful if you will. . . ."

"No, no," he cried, "I must speak. Ever since I have known you, the words I have to say have been on my lips, suffocating me. . . . Gilberte, Gilberte, I . . ."

She gave a desperate glance, the glance of a victim which does not know how to defend itself and awaits the blow that is about to fall. He stammered:

"Oh, your eyes . . . your eyes . . . !"

He remained on his knees, humble and undecided, and repeated, in a low voice:

"Your eyes . . . yes . . . my father told me . . . child's eyes that put one off . . ."

He rose and struck his fist upon the table:

"No, after all, I will not allow myself to be thwarted. I mean to speak and I shall speak. . . . If your eyes prevent me, well, I sha'n't see your eyes!"

He went to the lamp and, with a sudden movement, put it out.

Gilberte gave a scream. She tried to run away, stumbled over a chair and fell. She tried to call out; and her voice died away in her throat.

Then, powerless, she stirred no more.

He seized her hand and raised it to his lips.

She made a weak attempt to release herself, but strength failed her.

She said, simply:

"Please, monsieur . . . I have never done you any harm. . . . I have always been kind to you. . . . Please. . . ."

His hand slacked its grasp. They remained opposite each other. What was he going to say to her? At her wits' end, with her heart wildly beating, she tried, through the darkness, through the great, impenetrable silence that enshrouded the two of them, to see Simare's face, to read his tumultuous thoughts, his will. . . . A few seconds passed. . . .

Then he said:

"I beg your pardon. . . . I am a scoundrel. . . . I wanted to force you to take my name, to share my existence. . . . It was cowardly and base of me. . . . Still, there was more in me, believe me, than wicked designs. . . . Oh, I hear your heart beating . . . do not tremble! . . . You will never be in danger from any one . . . it is not only your eyes that protect you: there is the sound of your voice, there is your silence, there is the air you breathe, your mere presence. . . . Forgive me. . . ."

He went away. She dimly saw him cross the window-rail and presently heard the sound of his steps as he walked down the gravel-path in the garden.

Gilberte rushed to the door. She could

not have stayed for another instant in the solitude of that room.

It was an intolerable agony, of which she felt the grip even more now that Simare was no longer there. Where should she go? To Mme. de la Vaudraye's? She remembered vaguely that it was not one of her "evenings," because of the fair. No matter. She wanted people, lights, bustle, men and women in whose presence she could master her fears and pluck up courage.

She ran to her bedroom, put on her hat and cloak. . . . But no, she dared not go out. . . .

A noise came from the square in front of the Logis, on the town side; the noise of an altercation, of a struggle. She drew back the curtains. Two men were fighting under her windows. In her fright, she flew to the bolt, locked herself in and crouched down in the furthest corner of her room. Her instinct, her weakness impelled her to hide herself, to know nothing of what was happen-

ing, to wait. . . . But the din increased.
There were shouts and moans.

Then she was ashamed of her cowardice.
It was impossible for her to continue in that
nervous inactivity. She wanted to inter-
fere, to help, if there were still time.
Bravely, she opened the door, went down the
stairs, walked out into the square and up to
the combatants.

By the light of the lamp she recognized
Beaufrelant and Le Hourteulx.

Rolling on the ground, covered with mud,
hatless, their clothes all disarranged, they
were fighting with a sort of mad rage, with
the stubbornness of two mortal enemies re-
joicing in an opportunity of vengeance long
deferred. They struck at each other in
turns, collared each other, bashed each
other's faces with their fists, wrestled violently. And this amid insults and exclama-
tions of triumph:

"Here, you villain, take that!"

"One for you!"

"Ah, my fine fellow, you caught it this time!   How did that strike you?"

And they called Gilberte to witness, like the queen of a tournament in whose honour two of her knights were breaking a lance:

"What do you think of that, madame?"

"Got in there with my left, madame!"

"Ah, he was looking out for you, the scoundrel!"

"Oh, you blackguard, you were prowling round her house!"

Abandoning all attempts at interference, she turned to move away.   They rose with difficulty and followed her, each hustling his rival as he went on trying to get rid of him. But the heat of the struggle brought them to the ground again; and she ran away.

The first street to which her steps led her came out in front of the church.   The La Vaudrayes' house was close by; and she hastened to it.

No one answered when she rang the bell. Still, there was a light in the drawing-room.

She tapped at one of the windows. Some one came to the door. It was Guillaume de la Vaudraye.

"You, madame!" he exclaimed.

"Where's your mother? Where's your mother?" she panted.

"My mother is at Caen, on business; I am alone in the house."

She walked to the drawing-room unsteadily and sank into a chair.

"What is the matter? Why are you here?"

She whispered, in a broken voice:

"They came. . . . They are following me. . . . I am frightened of them. . . ."

"Simare, was it? . . . And Le Hourteulx, I suppose . . . and Beaufrelant. . . ."

"Yes . . . so I daren't go back. . . ."

"But Adèle . . . and her husband?"

"Gone to the fair."

He thought for a moment and said:

"I will go and fetch them. It's some way

off. Take a rest until we come: you need it."

Gilberte, utterly exhausted, fell asleep.

Adèle woke her. There was a taxi waiting for her. Guillaume did not show himself again.

VI

A NEW FRIEND

Two days later Domfront could not believe its ears when it heard that all relations had been broken off between the La Vaudrayes on the one hand and Beaufrelant and Le Hourteulx on the other. The two no longer formed part of the *salon*.

"Oh, nonsense! Beaufrelant and Le Hourteulx, who have been there longer than anybody, who date back to the days when the La Vaudrayes saw their friends at the Logis: it's impossible!"

"It's quite true, for all that. I heard it from Mme. Duval, who is constantly at all three houses; and she saw the letters which Mme. de la Vaudraye wrote."

"Well, you can say what you please, but

it's a great pity.   M. le Hourteulx: such a fine voice!   And M. Beaufrelant: such a brillant talker!   And have you heard the reason?"

"No, I can't imagine. . . . If I hear the least thing, I'll let you know."

Gilberte was very much vexed when Adèle told her what had happened.   She had no doubt that Guillaume de la Vaudraye had told his mother what he knew of the incident and she was distressed at being the cause of disagreement, complication and gossip.

"Perhaps," she thought, "all this would not have come about if I had not been looked upon as married."

And, as a matter of fact, she seemed, as a married woman, to be exposed to unpleasantness which she would have escaped in the position of a girl.   Instead of the quiet which she had sought, she found, in the men's behaviour, in their conversation, in their way of looking at her, in the persistency of their pursuit, a host of disturbing little annoyances which might well have troubled a mind less innocent than hers.

She went to Mme. de la Vaudraye, in the afternoon, and begged her to reconsider her decision.

"It is no use asking me," cried Mme. de la Vaudraye. "I admit that, in writing to those two gentlemen, I did no more than my duty; but it was my son who pointed out to me how imperative that duty was."

She was in a bad temper and, when all is said, with reason. No mistress of a house lightly gives up two individuals of the un-doubted merit of M. Beaufrelant and M. le Hourteulx. She called out:

"Guillaume, Mme. Armand wants to talk to you!"

And, when her son entered the room, she went out.

Gilberte, who was always frightened by Guillaume's obvious coldness and his exces-sive reserve, blushed as she made her request. Ought so much importance to be attached to an incident which the two gentlemen surely regretted and at which she could only laugh?

"My mother and I have no right to laugh at it," he said. "We are responsible for all the people whom we introduce to you. If one of them treats you with disrespect, we must not expose you to meeting him here."

"But how have they treated me with disrespect? . . . I assure you, I don't see it. . . ."

He looked at her, turned away his head and said, in a voice so abrupt that she could not make out whether his answer was full of contemptuous pity or affectionate admiration:

"It is the others, it is all of us who must see for you. . . . How can you be expected to see those things?"

He paused and continued:

"Are you very anxious to have those two boors back here?"

"For your mother's sake, yes. I feel that the situation grieves her."

"Why, of course," he exclaimed, with cutting irony, "they are the two finest ornaments of her *salon!* How will the others do without them? How will they manage to rattle out the regulation tomfoolery? Will they ever be able to reach the required level of absurdity, affectation, stupidity and narrowness? Heavens, if we were a shade less dull and less inane, what a catastrophe!"

"It's not right of you to talk like that, monsieur," said Gilberte.

"What!" he said, taken aback.

"No, you ought not to laugh at what is a great pleasure to your mother. If some of her friends are a little eccentric, it is not for you to remark upon it."

He rose, began to walk excitedly up and down the room and then, gradually mastering himself, came and sat opposite Gilberte again and said:

"You are right, madame. Besides, among all those people whom I cannot help criticizing, I have never heard you speak any but sensible, judicious, intelligent words, admirable for their kindness and wisdom. You always answer their most ridiculous questions as though they had asked you about the most interesting things in life. One word from you brings order and lucidity into the most absurd conversations."

It was no longer the same voice. Usually so hard and dictatorial, it had become humble and grave. And his face, which was generally severe, bore an expression of infinite gentleness. One was no longer conscious of acrimony, constraint or distrust, but of the frank unreserve of a pent-up nature and of subdued melancholy.

Which of the two was the real Guillaume? Gilberte did not even ask herself the question, was only too happy to believe at once in the more attractive of the two images presented to her. And so she smiled upon this second Guillaume and said:

"Then . . . those gentlemen . . . ?"

"Your two protégés shall resume the

places which they fill so well. I insist, however, on a temporary exclusion as a punishment; for it is a punishment to Le Hourteulx and Beaufrelant. After that, if they
are very good . . ."

"And you will be pleasant to them?"

"To them and to the others, at least as
pleasant as I can."

"Is it so very difficult?"

"Extremely! I can't help it: I do not
suffer fools gladly; they make me irritable
and unjust. I have not your charity."

"It only needs a little indulgence; think of
your mother."

"Oh, my mother, my mother!"

There was something sorrowful and harsh
about this exclamation that struck Gilberte.
She kept silence from a sense of delicacy.
But Guillaume was passing through one of
those periods when it is a relief to the over-
burdened soul to confess its troubles:

"Have my mother and I ever understood
each other? We have not an idea in com-

mon. Her wants are not mine, nor are mine hers. She offends all my tastes as I offend all hers. If I display so much bitterness against the merry-andrews who perform in her *salon*, it is because of her. I hate to see her countenancing their grimaces and posturings."

She said nothing. He asked:

"You blame me for it, don't you? Yes, yes, I feel it. . . . And how strange: in your presence, I too think that I am wrong and, while I was saying those things, I blushed as if I had uttered ugly thoughts!"

She laughed:

"They were not very pretty ones."

"Never mind, I prefer you to know them. I do not wish to trick you into liking me. If I ever win your esteem, I want to do so without hypocrisy, without trying to hide my faults from you."

No one had ever spoken to Gilberte with such seriousness and deference. She felt quite touched and, with a spontaneous movement, held out her hand to Guillaume:

"We shall be friends," she said. "I am sure that we shall be friends."

He was on the point of raising her small, gloved hand to his lips, but he restrained himself. And she went on:

"So this is the unsociable Guillaume de la Vaudraye! Will you believe that you quite frightened me with your surly ways? You did indeed!"

After this interview, Gilberte did two or three errands and returned to the Logis. It was drawing towards evening. She made for the summer-house and saw her dream-companion in the distance. She said to him, as though he could hear her and as though she felt bound to tell him the good news without delay:

"You know, I have a new friend!"

And Gilberte saw nothing extraordinary in this sudden friendship, based upon the exchange of a few sentences. Was she not one of those unsophisticated beings who al-

ways obey the unreflecting impulse of their
hearts, who look you straight in the eyes and
who do not think it out of place to tell people
how they feel towards them?

And so, the next evening, she went to
Mme. de la Vaudraye's, quite happy at the
thought of seeing her new friend again. A
disappointment awaited her: Guillaume did
not appear.

She went back next day. Guillaume
came down to the drawing-room, bowed to
her and seemed to take no further notice of
her presence.

Thereupon, on the third day, while the
others were listening to Mlle. du Bocage and
M. Lartiste the elder in the duet from *Mireille,* Gilberte, finding that Guillaume was
alone in the next room, went out to him.
She at once saw that he tried to avoid her.
Realizing this to be impossible, he gave a
gesture of vexation and crossed his arms in
an indifferent attitude.

"What about your promise?" she asked,

playfully, but a little sadly. "You promised to make yourself pleasant to your enemies in the *salon;* and this is the best you
can do! Am I not entitled to complain?
Did we not shake hands as friends?"

He uncrossed his arms and his expression
changed. Once again she felt the relaxation
of a tense will, the immediate suppression of
all resistance in this silent man whose square
chin and inflexible eyes bore witness to his
obstinacy.

"Good!" she said. "Capital! But you
still look a little fierce. . . . That's better! . . . And now, come along."

He stopped her:

"Do not ask too much of me. You are so
far above ordinary life, so inaccessible, that
you can mix with those people and remain
serene and untouched. I could only do so
at the risk of deteriorating. One must make
allowance for different temperaments. I
shall be polite, that's all."

Then she stayed and they talked.

Often, after that, Gilberte had to go to him and open, as she said, the door of his prison-house, unbind his hands and deliver his captive soul. But she did it so easily that it amused them both.

"You have but to lift your little finger," Guillaume would say, "to bring down the prison-walls."

Under this uneven and rugged husk, Gilberte discovered the most exquisite and delicate of natures, a poet's nature that was galled by all its surroundings, a child's nature that his mother had kept in to the verge of pain. And it was often from the point of view of a child that Gilberte was glad to be with him. They would laugh at the least thing, with that childish laughter, which is so good just because it has no excuse except our need of laughter. They longed to run and skip and play.

"Oh dear, how young I am!" Guillaume would exclaim.

"I shall be two next year," Gilberte declared.

They could be serious also. She asked him about his writing, wanted to read what he had printed. He refused, on the pretext that he was not satisfied. Nevertheless, he showed her a letter from the editor of an important review, a letter teeming with compliments.

He lent her his favorite books and she devoured them.

Mme. de la Vaudraye was in ecstasies. She was now certain that her dream would be realized. She was too clever to betray her delight and hid it under demonstrations of gratitude:

"How sweet of you, my dear Gilberte, to tame that wild savage! You will make quite a courtier of him."

And she added, with a sigh:

"Oh, if you could only turn him into a more attentive son and make him more

grateful to his mother for all the sacri-
fices she has made for him!"

The discord between Mme. de la Vaudraye and Guillaume was Gilberte's greatest
grief. Her love of harmony prompted her
to make continual endeavours at reconcilia-
tion which were bound to fail as much because of the mother's arid artificiality as of
the son's stubbornness and reserve.

She had to give up the attempt.

But she suffered another pain, arising
from her extreme sensitiveness: at the close
of day, she could no longer go to the ruined
summer-house without a certain sense of dis-
comfort. Her unknown friend was faith-
ful to the daily tryst which they had made
with their dreams; and, though Gilberte herself never failed to keep it, she felt as though
she had done him some wrong. With her
eyes fixed on the distant mountains melting
into the deep blue of the heavens, she let
herself drift into vague reveries, far, very far
away from the homely valley where her first

friend patiently waited for her thoughts to
return to him. It was at such times, when
the darkness overtook her amidst this delightful torpor, that she seemed to be coming
back from a long journey. She was almost
angry with herself. But why? She could
not have said.

One day, at five o'clock, as she was going
down to her garden, she received a note from
Mme. de la Vaudraye.

"MY DEAR GILBERTE,
"Guillaume and I are going for a stroll in
the Forest of Andaine. It is such a fine
evening: do come with us."

Should she go? To do so meant a break
in sweet custom that had lent such charm to
the most oppressive hours of her life, meant
throwing over the constant friendship of the
bad days.

She wavered and, wavering, went up to
her room, put on her things, went out and
knocked at the La Vaudrayes' door.

Whatever regrets may have lingered in her conscientious mind were very soon dispelled by the pleasure which the walk gave her from the start.   Spring was trying her hand, at the tips of the branches, with tiny pale-green leaves and, along the roadsides and ditches, with those charming early flowers which are so dear to us: anemones, periwinkles, primroses, wild hyacinths, lilies of the valley. . . . Arched lanes sped into the depths of the woods.   Sweet scents, songs and colours played and mingled in all the gladness of new-born nature.

They walked without speaking.   Sometimes, Guillaume and Gilberte would point out to each other, with a glance, a corner of the landscape, or the outline of a tree, or the glint of a ray of sunshine, both wishing the other to share their delight and admiration.

They sat down on the edge of a pool whose waters slumbered amidst a circle of old pines that joined their arms around them as though to dance a moveless measure.   It was one of those abodes of silence that open only in the hearts of old forests. Those who are brought there by chance and who grasp the fitness of things are themselves silent.

Mme. de la Vaudraye exclaimed:

"On the first fine Sunday, we must make up a party and come here. It is a lovely spot for a picnic. What do you say?"

They did not reply. She continued:

"Every one will bring his own provisions. Of course, Mme. Charmeron will make her famous spiced beef and Mlle. du Bocage her prune-tart. And, at dessert, everybody must come out with a set of verses!"

Guillaume hurled a pebble violently into the mirror of the water.

"What's the matter with you?" asked Mme. de la Vaudraye.

He sprang up and confronted her, angrily, impatiently, with tense wrists. But, as he was about to speak, he met Gilberte's eyes, sad and full of entreaty. He seemed quite dazed, his lips trembled and suddenly

he took Mme. de la Vaudraye in his arms
and began to kiss her with all his might, with
all his fervent soul.   And he blurted out:

"It's quite right . . . you're my mother
. . . you're my mother . . . you're entitled
to say what you please. . . . What you say
is right. . . . It's my business to understand. . . . Oh, mother, if you only
knew . . . !"

VII

GILBERTE'S TWO FRIENDS

GILBERTE did not go to the summer-house again. A feeling of delicacy kept her away. Nevertheless, each day, at the accustomed hour, something like a light cloud passed over her mind; and she was not far from accusing herself of ingratitude.

What was but a vague remorse towards a friend whom she had never known took a more definite shape, in another sense, with regard to him whom she now saw almost daily. She would so much have liked to offer him a brand-new friendship and to feel the excitement of it for the first time! True, there was no struggle between two sentiments, since one was so far-off and vague, the other so vivid and distinct. And yet . . .

There are childish conflicts which would not even ripple the most scrupulous soul, but which form the mighty storms of peaceful and innocent consciences such as Gilberte's.

But all this took place deep down within herself, unconsciously, so to speak, and could not diminish her magical delight in living. For magic it was, something that approached a miracle, when she compared the gloom of the past with the dazzling life of the present. Whence did she derive the joy with which she thrilled at her awakening; the enthusiasm that swept her at the sight of a flower, of a landscape, of any spectacle a hundred times witnessed and never fully seen; that exaltation of thought, those sudden blushes, that inexplicable torpor of her whole being and, at the same time, that unchangeable serenity which doubled the uncertainty of her life with strength, faith, patience and certainty?

There was no allusion to the incident in

the Forest of Andaine.   But, from that time onward, Mme. de la Vaudraye looked upon her son in a different fashion; and, in the same way, in her conduct towards Gilberte, there was something that had hitherto been lacking: a touch of respect.

Guillaume said to Gilberte:

"You are a regular fairy, no, more than a fairy, for you exercise your power without knowing or trying.   To do good, to disarm hatred, to heal wounds, to make others want to be indulgent and kind, you have no need even to wish.   You have only to be as you are; and everything around you grows nobler and better."

She listened and smiled.   From him she accepted praise without blushing.   He could have praised her beauty and enumerated all her charms without causing her to lower her eyes.   He could not wound her maidenly modesty.

One morning, following upon a day when

Gilberte had not been to Mme. de la Vaudraye's, Adèle came back from the town all
out of breath:

"Oh, ma'am, here's a nice to do! Yesterday, at Mme. de la Vaudraye's evening,
young M. Simare . . ."

"I thought he was away," said Gilberte,
interrupting her.

"He is back; and, last evening, he and M.
Guillaume, during the duet from *Mireille,*
had some words in a corner . . . they were
heard quarrelling. . . . It seems that the
elder M. Simare told a story that wasn't
quite proper and M. Guillaume went for the
son about it."

"Oh, it's all my fault!" said Gilberte to
herself, feeling certain that Guillaume had
taken the first opportunity to bring about a
rupture.

And she asked:

"Is that all?"

"Yes. Mme. Duval saw two officers ring-
ing at the Simares' house just now and she

says that M. Guillaume has ordered the landau from the hotel for presently . . . but that has nothing to do with it."

Though she did not foresee the possible consequences of an altercation between the two young men, Gilberte was convinced that no interference on her part would settle things, as it had done with M. le Hourteulx and M. Beaufrelant. Guillaume would not consent to have M. Simare admitted to the house again. The father would side with his son. Mme. de la Vaudraye would be furious at losing two of her regular visitors. In short, it meant a whole series of bothers and quarrels, of which Gilberte would have been the real cause.

She was very low-spirited at lunch. A presentiment of danger depressed her, but she could not have said of what sort it was nor whom it threatened.

Her suffering must have been genuine to induce her to rise suddenly, go out and turn her steps towards the La Vaudrayes' house.

But what she was doing must also have
seemed to her very useless and very serious
to make her stop suddenly, with frightened
hesitation. How was she to act? Whom
was she to influence? What events was she
to avert?

The church was near and she went in.
But she was unable to pray; and her anxiety became all the more painful inasmuch as
she did not know its reason. Then, rather
than return to the Logis, where inactivity
would have been intolerable, she went along
the high-road to the bottom of the valley,
followed the Varenne for a short distance
and then climbed up towards the Haute-
Chapelle.

At three o'clock, feeling a little tired, she
made for the shade on the skirt of a little
wood and sat down. She had hardly left the
road when the hotel landau passed and
turned down the forest-lane. Was Guillaume in it?

A sound of harness-bells, the crack of a

whip told her that another carriage was on its way. A break came dashing along, carrying Simare and a couple of officers, and disappeared down the same lane.

For a second, Gilberte stood breathless at a horrible thought. She would not, no, she would not have it! Then, suddenly, she began to run at full speed. A cross-roads brought her to a stop forthwith. Which of the three roads should she take?

She chose the one on the right, but, after running fifty yards, went back to the middle one and then to the one on the left. After that, she roamed at random, beating the copses, hunting on the grass for the marks of carriage-wheels, flinging herself among the ferns, listening and looking with all her nerves on edge. . . .

A shot . . . and a second, at almost the same moment . . . close by. . . .

She gave a scream and fell to the ground.

A few minutes passed. As though in a dream, she saw, through the branches, the two carriages driving by. Then voices sounded:

"I assure you, doctor, I am not mistaken. It was a woman screaming."

She had not the strength to raise her eyelids or speak; but she felt that two men were coming towards her. One of them bent over her and took her hand:

"It's nothing. She has only fainted."

"In that case, doctor, don't wait," said the other voice. "I will see her home."

The mist in which she was struggling lifted slowly. She perceived the smell of the earth on which she lay. She made an effort to throw off the feeling of sleep that numbed her and she opened her eyes. Guillaume was standing before her.

"You, you?" she whispered. "Oh, how glad I am! And M. Simare?"

"He's not hurt either."

"That's a good thing."

There was a pause; and then she asked:

"Why did you do it? It was not right."

"I lost my head, when he spoke to me last night, and I yielded to an irresistible impulse of hatred.   I did not know what I was doing."

"But your mother?"

"I have managed to hide the truth from her so far.   One of my seconds said that he would tell her."

"Go to her, run as fast as you can. . . . She will be so anxious until she sees you. . . . Go at once. . . ."

"No."

He was so firm that she despaired of persuading him.   And yet she wanted him to go.   Then she looked at him and smiled:

"To please me," she said.

"Very well," he said, "but you must come too."

She at once summoned her pluck and rose to her feet; and, when she expressed her wish to get back without delay he led her through the short cuts where there was hardly room to walk side by side.   But their pace slackened at once; and they stopped three times to rest on the road. Gilberte no longer displayed any hurry. What did they say? Nothing but insignificant words, which they did not remember afterwards. Nevertheless, when uttering them, they felt that they had never been interested in weightier matters. What importance could suddenly have attached, in the course of a walk, to the sight of two initials interlaced on the bark of a tree, or to the flight of a bird, or to a stone rolling down a slope! Whereas, to them, these were so many astounding incidents that deserved a stop and the interchange of a few ecstatic words.

A contest between some insect and a squad of five ants that were trying to drag it away kept them for quite a long time. Who would be the victor? Gilberte took pity on the insect and saved it when it was on the point of falling in the fray. Guillaume exclaimed, in accents of profound conviction:

"You are the most generous-hearted creature I have ever met."

Guillaume compared the moss at the foot of an oak to velvet; and Gilberte became aware that all the poetry in the world was summed up in her companion.

Having exhausted their original reflexions, their brilliant remarks and their mutual admiration, they were silent until they emerged from the wood. A lane of apple-trees led them past furze and rocks. At the foot of the slope ran the Varenne. After they had taken a turn, Gilberte cried:

"Look, that might be my garden, on the other side. . . . Why, so it is! . . . There's the Logis. . . . Where are we?"

She walked on. They came to a cluster of small fir-trees. When they had passed them, they were just opposite the ruined summer-house, with only the width of the valley in between.

Gilberte gave a start. That spur of the hill, that circle of red rocks surrounding it, that cluster of firs: was this not the spot where the unknown stranger, for months . . . ?

A flood of contradictory feelings welled up within her: feelings of gratitude towards the invisible friend, feelings of confusion towards the actual friend, memories of the dear past and visions of the present. How she wished that she had not come to this place with Guillaume! She felt inclined to exclaim:

"Go away! Go away!"

But, on turning her head, she was stupefied at the sight of his pallor and the change in his face:

"What's the matter? Why don't you say something? Speak to me!"

She broke off. A sudden thought struck her, an improbable, but madly delightful idea. She fixed her eyes on his, looked down into his very soul; and the truth appeared to her so clearly that, leaning against the side of the rock, she gasped:

"It was you all the time! . . . It was you! . . ."

Not for a moment did the shadow of a fear that she was mistaken, cross her. Holding her head between her hands and closing her eyes, she took refuge in her happiness as in an inaccessible dwelling from which not even he could have driven her.

He was speaking now, kneeling before her; and it seemed to Gilberte as though two voices were joined in that one voice of entreaty, as though the unknown friend were joining his prayer to Guillaume's, blending his image with Guillaume's, mingling with him and beseeching her with the same hands, adoring her with the same heart:

"Gilberte, it was the day on which you arrived at Domfront. You were in the public gardens, near the ruins, and I saw you raise your mourning-veil. Since that day, my life has been wrapped up in yours. When you went over the Logis with my mother, I was there, hiding behind a curtain. You stopped close by me, I was able to take you in my eyes, to lock you in my breast like a treasure; I heard your voice, I breathed your fragrance and I lived on that memory for weeks, seeking you, calling you, hovering round the Logis, hoping for a chance meeting.   Oh, the delight of it when I saw you from here, one afternoon, and when you came back next day and every day, every day!   I was not sure, but it appeared to me that you saw me . . . and then . . . that it was just a little because of me that you came back."

"I saw you, yes, I saw you," said Gilberte, without removing her clasped hands from her face.

He asked:

"Are you crying?"

"I am so happy!"

"Happy?"

"Yes, happy because it was you."

"Gilberte," he begged, "I would give worlds to see your tears."

She showed her dear face all wet with tears, all smiling with tears. He whispered:

"I love you."

She seemed surprised and repeated, gravely:

"You love me . . . you love me . . ."

He watched her anxiously. But the bright features lit up anew and she said to Guillaume, gaily and blithely, as though she had made the most wonderful and unexpected of discoveries:

"But, you know, Guillaume, I love you too."

She had the look of a delighted child. She could have clapped her hands, so great was the enchantment of that magnificent vision of love, so sweet was it to know that she loved and was loved.

She leant over to him prettily:

"Then you are the one I was loving all the time and it is you that I love, Guillaume?"

"Gilberte . . . please . . ."

"What do you want?   Tell me what you want, Guillaume."

"Your eyes, Gilberte, to kiss your innocent eyes, your eyes which are like the eyes of a little girl."

Closing the lids, she offered her eyes, as though it were a quite natural thing.   He took her in his arms and drew her to him. But a shiver passed through her at once. She made an instinctive movement of resistance and moaned:

"No . . . no . . . oh, please don't! . . ."

She was not laughing now.   A blush covered her cheeks and forehead.   She no longer dared look at him; and Guillaume's eyes almost hurt her.   This time, it was the real, perturbing, mysterious revelation of love.   Shaken with emotion, she faltered:

"Go away . . . please go away . . ."

He kissed the hem of her skirt, picked some leaves, some blades of grass that Gilberte's feet had trodden and went away.

VIII

THE APPOINTMENT

"GILBERTE:

"I must not see you again. When you read these lines, I shall have left Domfront. You are rich and I am poor: you need look for no other explanation of my departure and of my conduct in the past. I loved you from the first; and from the first I swore that I would shun you and for ever conceal the feeling with which you inspire me.

"Do you now understand why I behaved so coldly to you from the beginning, though my heart throbbed at the mere sound of your voice; why I was so hard to my mother, whose plans were obvious to all and drove me to exasperation: I was afraid lest you should think that I was privy to them; why I kept in the background, hiding among those rocks, looking at you from a distance as at a goal which I knew was, and wished it to be, inaccessible?

"But you came to me, Gilberte: that is all my excuse.   You came to me out of kindness to my mother, perhaps also prompted by that instinct which makes us conscious of love where it lies deepest.   What could I do against your fascination?   I did not even struggle.   I closed my eyes to all that was not you, you and your beauty and your smile and your charming grace and the colour of your hair and the freshness of your cheeks and the rhythm of your footsteps; and, with not a further thought of my oath or the inevitable consequences of my weakness, I accepted the infinite joy that came to me.   Oh, Gilberte, those few weeks! . . . But there was something which I had never imagined in my boldest dreams: you loved me, you also loved me.

"You love me, which means that happiness is within my reach to-morrow, the next

day, every day.   It is there, I have but to
take it; a word from me and you are my wife.
For I know you, my beloved: the gift of
your heart is the gift of your entire life.

"And so I must go, if I would not be overcome by temptation . . .

"Oh, Gilberte, you do not know what I
am feeling and suffering, you who do not
know what you are, you who are all that is
most human and most divine, most noble
and most simple, a miracle of harmony, at-
tractiveness and light.   But you know nothing of yourself and will never know anything.   One could tell you and your mirror
could teach you all the perfections of your
face and form; and yet you would not know
them.   Were you a child of ten, wearing the
white frock of your first communion, I
should proclaim my admiration with the
same frankness and with no greater fear of
hurting your modesty.   The whole world
might be at your feet, chanting your praises;
and you would be none the less humble.

That is the marvel of your ingenuous nature. All is merged in your purity, as in a great, limpid sea in which every impurity would vanish. It is impossible to think of you without evoking images of whiteness, of transparency, of crystal water. By what mystery has it come that the trials of life, the realities of marriage have not soiled the freshness of your innocent eyes?

"And so I shall never see your eyes again: your eyes of the dawn, your eyes fresh as the dew, your kind, ignorant, gentle eyes, so fond, so gay, so sad . . ."

She lowered her head, overcome with emotion. Mme. de la Vaudraye, who had brought her this letter from her son and who waited for her to finish reading it, said, rather aggressively:

"I should be glad of a word of explanation, Gilberte. Yesterday, my son fights a duel without any adequate cause. To-day, he leaves me, without giving me any reason.

Have these two incidents anything to do
with you? You must admit their seriousness to a mother."

Gilberte handed her the letter. Mme. de
la Vaudraye read it and shrugged her shoulders:

"Are you so very rich?"

The girl gave her another letter, received that morning, in which the Dieppe
solicitor furnished her with her quarterly
statement. Mme. de la Vaudraye started:

"Impossible! Oh, my child, you must
never let Guillaume know!"

"How can I? He has gone away!"

"And you sit there and say that so
quietly! Doesn't his going distress you?
Don't you love him?"

"Yes, I love him."

"Then write to him."

"Write to him?"

"Yes, tell him to come back . . . tell him
that his position makes no difference to
you . . ."

She spoke with a certain embarrassment; and this made Gilberte feel awkward. However, she said:

"I can't write. Guillaume alone can solve the question that lies between him and his conscience."

Mme. de la Vaudraye gave an impatient gesture and cried:

"You can't write! What a ridiculous scruple! Is it any worse to write to a young man than to go walking about the country with him, as I hear you did yesterday? What! My son fights a duel because of you, he leaves me because of you; and, when I, his mother, ask you . . . ! Well, what's the matter? What are you looking at me like that for?"

A chair suddenly pushed aside, an over-turned flower-vase bore evidence to Mme. de la Vaudraye's burst of irritation. She flew out again:

"Oh, yes, it's all very well, but one can't stand that eternal gentleness of yours!

Here am I, telling you how wrong you are, and you listen in such a queer way that I end by putting myself in the wrong. One always feels with you as though one were in front of an indulgent judge, who graciously forgives one's faults. And yet it's you who are at fault!"

"Why, of course!" said Gilberte, all confusion.

"Then why do I look like a prisoner being judged?"

"Oh, but you don't!"

"Yes, I do. It's all very well for you to bend your head and all very well for me to rave and yell: any one would think that I was to blame and that you were making allowances. You must admit, it is enough to make one lose all patience."

Presumably, Mme. de la Vaudraye was afraid of growing still more impatient, for she went away without another word.

Gilberte called on her, next day, and kissed her affectionately. There was not a word said about their difference of the day before.

They saw each other every day. According to the weather, they walked in the town or walked about the neighbourhood, leaning on each other's arm and heedless of any but themselves. But they invariably returned at the same hour.

"Ah, it's five o'clock: here are the ladies coming back!" people said.

This regularity was due to Gilberte. As soon as she was free, she went to the ruined summer-house and sat there until dinner-time.

"But why this hurry?" asked Mme. de la Vaudraye. "You never give me a minute over."

"And what about my daily appointment?" said Gilberte, laughing.

"Your appointment?"

"Why, yes, with your son: what would he think of me if I were not punctual?"

In the course of a longer excursion than

usual, Mme. de la Vaudraye, who was fond
of turning the conversation on her past
greatness, pointed out the limits of the property once possessed by her ancestors.   They
extended along both banks of the Varenne,
as far as the spot where it joined the An-
dainette.

"To say nothing of what we owned on the
forest side: the Revolution robbed us of that.
Why, on the death of my father, the whole
of the valley still belonged to us! My mar-
riage-portion included everything down to
the Bas-Moulin.   And you should have seen
the Logis in those days! Such furniture!
Such works of art!"

Gilberte, to humour her, asked:

"And how did you lose it?"

"Oh, it's a long story, a heap of mysterious business-schemes in which my poor husband, a decent man, if ever there was one,
allowed himself to be robbed by a company-
promoter called Despriol. You remember
that empty house, near Notre-Dame-sur-

l'Eau, which took your fancy yesterday, I
don't quite know why? Well, that's where
Despriol and his wife lived, up to fifteen
years ago. Henriette Despriol was a
charming woman; she and I were great
friends; and she used to come to the Logis
when she liked . . . so did her husband, for
M. de la Vaudraye was never happy out of
his sight; and I did not dream of suspecting
him, for he struck me as a good-natured, hon-
est man and M. de la Vaudraye was careful
to hide from me the dangerous speculations
into which his evil genius was dragging him.
Everything was discovered in an hour.
Despriol took to flight, after losing, or rather
stealing, all that remained to us. We were
ruined."

She paused and then continued:

"There's worse than that. On the same
evening, my dear friend Henriette came and
flung herself on her knees before me and im-
plored me to give her money to join her husband, who was in concealment in the neigh-

bourhood, and to enable them to leave the country and retrieve their fortunes.   It was a piece of brazen impudence; and I showed her the door.   Unfortunately, I left her alone, for a moment, in my bedroom.   An hour after, I saw that a box containing all my jewels had disappeared.   We rushed to her house: she was gone."

"Did you prosecute them?"

"We notified the police, but they were never found.   Five years ago, I received a letter from Henriette in which she said, 'The ten thousand francs which my husband sent you this morning represent the value of the jewels.   It is the first money which we have been able to put by.   I am longing for the day when we shall be in a position to settle with you altogether and when I shall have the right to beg your forgiveness for all the harm that we have done you.   Until that day comes there will be no rest for your repentant friend."

"And since then . . .?"

"Since then, I have received another letter, a few months ago, in which she told me
that her husband was dead and that she was
on her way to me with all the money she
owed me."

"Well?"

"Nothing but lies! Nobody came. Do
people like that come and pay back the
money they have stolen! No, they were a
couple of thieves. You ask anybody at
Domfront about M. and Mme. Despriol: a
nice reputation they left behind them! If
either of them thought of coming back here,
they'd be stoned in the streets! Henriette
indeed! Why, I should spit in her face,
that I would, the sneak, the hypocrite! . . ."

She uttered those words with an accent of
implacable hatred charged with all the ran-
cour of those fifteen years of poverty and
privation. Gilberte shuddered. The evil
expression on that face filled her with a sort
of repugnance. Nevertheless, she took

Mme. de la Vaudraye's hand and, raising it
to her lips, murmured:

"You poor dear!"

And she did this not designedly, because
it was Guillaume's mother whom she was
conciliating, but from an undefined and all-
powerful instinct that compelled her to be
kind to this humiliated and disappointed
woman.

It was the same instinct which had guided
her hitherto and which made her still more
attentive and affectionate in the days that
followed, notwithstanding a certain sense
of constraint which she felt in Mme. de la
Vaudraye's presence.   She knew no greater
pleasure than to smooth the wrinkles from
those sullen features at the moment when
they were most firmly set; and to do this she
employed all sorts of childish rogueries:

"Come, try hard and laugh. . . . There,
you have laughed!"

Mme. de la Vaudraye was touched by all

this charm of manner. It made her neglect
the artificial plan of conduct which she had
arranged to captivate the girl: she forgot
to conceal her faults, she even became natural and spontaneous.

One day, after something that Gilberte
had said, with a sudden movement she drew
the girl to her:

"Oh, my darling, what a treasure of a
wife you would make!"

Gilberte smiled:

"Indeed! How do I know that you would
have me for a daughter! . . . However, we
shall soon see . . . perhaps to-morrow . . ."

"To-morrow?"

"Why, of course! Isn't this the day when
Guillaume is coming to the trysting-place
where I wait for him every day?"

"Guillaume? I had a letter from him this
morning from Paris. Besides, I know him:
when he has made up his mind . . ."

Gilberte looked at her watch:

"Five o'clock. Suppose he were there

now! . . . Ah, I have a feeling that he is there to-day, that I shall see him! . . . Good-bye till to-morrow."

She hastened away swiftly, leaving her companion speechless. Hope filled her breast, a hope each time disappointed, but never discouraged.

"Mme. Armand is coming back alone this afternoon," said the people at Domfront. "What a hurry she's in!"

She crossed the threshold of the Logis without stopping and went straight to the summer-house. Her eyes longed to pierce the screen of foliage that hid the hill from sight. She had not a doubt that he was there; and, at the same time, she felt the madness of her certainty.

She arrived. Her glance at once swept the rocks. He was there.

She was on the point of throwing him handfuls of kisses, or else of kneeling down and stretching out her arms to him across space, but she saw him running down the

slope and she herself started running towards him, as fast as she could.

She arrived all out of breath at the bottom
of the garden, broke down the little wooden
gate, which was slow in opening, and sprang
into the road at the moment when Guillaume
crossed the bridge:

"Gilberte!"

"Guillaume!"

They assured themselves with a glance
that nothing was changed in either of them
and then silently followed the road that
skirts the Varenne.   They dared not speak,
overcome with the importance of the words
which they were about to pronounce.   Besides, excitement gripped them by the
throat.

Thus they arrived at Notre-Dame-sur-
l'Eau, the old Norman chapel which is so
prettily situated on the river-bank.

Leaning on the balustrade above the
water flowing through the arches of the
bridge, they revelled in the delight of dream-

ing side by side. Then Guillaume said:

"It was more than I could bear. I wanted to see you, if only for a few minutes . . . and to gather fresh courage . . ."

She asked, in a voice that did not sound like her own:

"Then . . . you are going back? . . ."

"I intended to . . . but I can't now . . . I can't now . . ."

He continued, almost in a whisper:

"It's not weakness. But I am seeing you; and to see you is to see things and ideas as they are. You flood them with the light which is in you and which springs from you. Yes, I tried to escape the temptation and I had a wild desire to work in solitude, so as to achieve the wealth and fame that would have permitted me to marry you. And now . . . and now I see that it is all madness. Why suffer uselessly? Let us struggle together, Gilberte. I can do nothing without you . . . I am too much in love with you."

"And your scruples?" she asked, maliciously.

"What do wealth and poverty matter? They are words to which I was able to attach a certain value when away from you in writing to you.   But, when I am near you, it seems to me that they mean nothing.   A man has no right to order his life by such empty phrases. . . . Oh, Gilberte, you put everything in its right proportion, you are truth itself, your love gives certainty and peace!   Such as I am, I am worthy of you, because you love me . . ."

She gave him her hand.   He asked:

"You are not angry with me?"

"For going away, Guillaume?   No, I was so sure that you would come back!"

IX

On the next afternoon, Adèle burst into the room where Gilberte was sitting after lunch:

"M'am, there's Mme. de la Vaudraye and her son turning into the square. Am I to let them in?"

"Yes, certainly, I am expecting them."

"Then it's true what Mme. Duval says, that you're going to marry M. Guillaume, ma'am?"

"Well, suppose I am?"

"Oh, as far as M. Guillaume's concerned, I've nothing to say! But Mme. de la Vaudraye as your mother-in-law! If you want to know, ma'am, I'd rather . . ."

The front-bell rang; and she went to the door looking very cross.

Gilberte shot a glance at the glass over the mantel-piece, pushed a curl into place and nervously made a change in the flowers in the vases, bunches of roses which she had gathered herself. Adèle showed in the mother and son.

Mme. de la Vaudraye was radiant. A moment before, in the main street, the mere sight of her silk dress, her ceremonious walk and her triumphant expression must have told the inhabitants of Domfront the exact nature of her errand.

She entered with the ease of one who is quite at home. Her way of sitting down showed that she was definitely and blissfully taking possession. There was none of the stiffness, none of the preliminary commonplaces that usually mark this sort of interview. Mme. de la Vaudraye was much too eager to come to the point:

"My dear Gilberte, I wish to ask your hand for my son Guillaume."

All their love, all the unspeakable happi-

ness of their souls, all their gratitude, all
their faith in the future was contained in
the glance exchanged by Guillaume and Gilberte. Nothing remained of the irritation
which his mother's air of victory caused him,
nothing remained of the anxiety which the
other felt at this solemn hour.

Mme. de la Vaudraye did not even wait
to hear the answer.

"First of all, my dear child, let me speak
to you as a friend and as a woman of experience, who knows only too well, by what she
herself has been through, that happiness in
married life is based upon material prosperity. You know, don't you, how Guillaume
and I are placed as regards money? On the
death of my poor husband . . ."

Guillaume rose and walked to the open
window, as though bored beforehand by what
was coming. Gilberte felt very much inclined to join him and to leave Mme. de la
Vaudraye to fight out with herself the question of the material prosperity on which

married bliss is based. But the older woman's imperious eye nailed her to her chair; and, nodding her head at intervals, by way of assent, she had to listen to a long speech in which strange phrases like separate and common property, joint estate and settlements kept on recurring.

"That will do nicely," she said, with an air of deliberation, though she did not understand a single word of what was said.

"Are we agreed?"

"Quite, madame."

"Well, children, kiss each other and bless you!"

Guillaume stepped forward and his outstretched arms closed round Gilberte. He kissed her forehead, kissed her eyes. She released herself, blushing, and said:

"It is my first kiss, Guillaume."

He felt a momentary bitterness:

"Your first . . . from me."

She smiled:

"A girl must not receive a kiss from any

but the man she is engaged to . . . and are you not the first, the only one?"

"What do you mean, Gilberte?"

"I mean, Guillaume," she said, in accents throbbing with her heart's gladness, "I mean that I am not a widow, that I have never been married, that I called myself a married woman in the hope of escaping attention and that no such person as Mme. Armand exists."

Guillaume was trembling with emotion. He understood, yet refused to admit the truth, so great would have been the anguish of a mistake:

"No, no, I dare not believe it . . . you, a girl, unmarried!"

"What is there so extraordinary in that?"

"Oh, Gilberte!"

He had seized her hands and stood gazing at her in ecstasy.

She whispered:

"I was sure that you would be delighted."

"It is something more than delight. You

seem to me even more beautiful and even more innocent and sacred. I do not love you any better, but I love you differently."

And he continued:

"Is it really possible? Is there no one in your past? Is there not even that shadow on my happiness?"

"My whole past is you, Guillaume."

Mme. de la Vaudraye came up to them. They had forgotten all about her; and her appearance gave them an impression that was all the more painful inasmuch as the sudden gravity of her features was in direct contrast with their own rapture. She said to Gilberte:

"If Mme. Armand does not exist, then whom is my son marrying?"

"Well, Gilberte . . ."

"Gilberte whom?"

"Gilberte Me," replied the girl, trying to speak playfully, but half-uneasy at heart.

"Come, child, that's not enough. You must have a surname? . . ."

"I suppose so . . ."

"What was your father's name? Your mother's?"

"I don't know."

Mme. de la Vaudraye drew herself up to the full length of her angular figure. It was as though she were learning some terrible event, a catastrophe. Gilbert caught sight of Guillaume's pallor and suddenly understood what she had never even half-realized, the danger of her irregular position where a woman like Mme. de la Vaudraye was concerned. She shook with terror.

Guillaume interposed gently:

"Don't upset yourself, Gilberte. I need not say how little importance I attach to all this; but mother does not look at things from my point of view. Let us hear the facts."

Gilberte, without entering into details, told of the death of her mother, the loss of the family-papers and the whole chapter of accidents which had prevented her from penetrating the mystery that surrounded

her.   As she went on, her voice lost its as-
surance.   All this story, which, until then,
she had simply regarded as a source of petty
worries, now, under Mme. de la Vaudraye's
stern eye, appeared to her the abominable
story of a worthless creature.   To be without a name!   She felt as much ashamed of
herself as though they had made the unexpected discovery that she had an ear missing,
or a piece of one cheek.   And yet, in the
silence that followed on her recital she
sought in vain for the crime which she had
committed, for the crime of which she was
held guilty.

"Well, mother," said Guillaume, "there's
nothing serious in that."

"Nothing serious!" sneered Mme. de la
Vaudraye.

All her little middle-class, provincial feelings were outraged by this unforeseen revelation.   The pride of the La Vaudrayes cried
aloud within her.   What would people say
at Domfront if a La Vaudraye married a

girl without a name, a foundling, an adventuress, in fact! She pictured the tittletattle, the sidelong allusions, the condolences with which she would be overwhelmed.

"My poor friend, how very unpleasant for you! . . . Of course, I knew there was something suspicious about her, for, after all . . ."

And they would say, among themselves:

"No name? Nonsense! When people haven't a name, it's because it's to their interest not to have one, because they are hiding their real name."

She did not take the trouble to put it politely. Bluntly, she declared:

"The marriage is out of the question. It will not take place."

Guillaume protested indignantly:

"Out of the question! And why, pray?"

"Can't you see that for yourself? I'm surprised at your asking!"

"I insist on knowing, as Gilberte's affianced husband."

"Gilberte's   husband! People   don't
marry . . ."

"Silence, mother!"

He was standing before her, with his features convulsed. Another word and he
would have closed her lips by mean force.
She was afraid of him. He went on, drop-
ping his voice:

"You are right, we had better not continue this explanation in her presence. Any
words other than words of veneration I look
upon as an insult to the girl I love."

He pushed her towards the door sternly.
But Gilberte barred their road:

"No, Guillaume, not like that. . . . If we
must part, let it not be with angry words.
. . . I love both of you too well, yes, both
of you, madame," she declared, in the voice
that no one could resist.

Her gentleness was stronger than Guillaume's violence. He made no further
movement. Mme. de la Vaudraye allowed
herself to be led back into the room. Gil-

berte made her sit down and knelt beside
her:

"Act as your conscience tells you, but,
please, without any bitterness against me.
. . . Whatever you decide to do, do not let
me lose your affection."

There may have been a sort of revenge on
Gilberte in Mme. de la Vaudraye's unbend-
ing attitude. She rejoiced to see this child,
who had always dominated her by her goodness and candour, on her knees before her,
while she, the judge, looked down from her
moral pedestal and put her to confusion from
the heights of her respectability.

She did not reply. Gilberte continued:

"You remember our walk, a little while
ago, when you showed me the former boun-
daries of your property. . . . Well, I
bought it all up . . . in order to give it back
to you. I hoped to bring you back here,
to this house which belongs to you. Everything is yours, you would have managed
and disposed of everything, you would have

been the absolute mistress, answerable to
no one, you would have resumed your
proper place at Domfront, the Logis would
have become what it used to be . . ."

A gleam flashed through Mme. de la
Vaudraye's eyes, but she restrained herself.
The same inflexible will contracted her face
into a hard and stiff mask. Coldly, she
said:

"I am exceedingly sorry that all these fine
plans cannot be realized, but it is not my
fault. . . . Make enquiries. . . . Who knows?
. . . Perhaps you will succeed in finding
out the indispensable truth."

Gilberte, in her despair, was nearly flinging her arms round her neck and saying:

"Stay here, please. . . . Be to me the
mother whom I have lost. . . . I will love
you like a daughter . . ."

But Guillaume prevented her:

"Why humiliate yourself, Gilbert? . . .
If my mother will not consent . . ."

"Well?"

"Well, are we not free?"

"No, Guillaume," she answered, firmly, "I will not marry you except with your mother's entire approval."

He turned pale and murmured:

"But . . . we shall see each other . . ."

"We shall not see each other. We can only see each other by stealth; and that is unworthy of us."

"Suppose I meet you . . ."

"I shall not leave the Logis."

"But . . ."

"We will wait, Guillaume. Am I not your promised bride?"

He bowed. His mother went out. He followed her.

And Gilberte felt as though she had never been so lonely in her life.

X

THE DESERTED HOUSE

NEXT day, Gilberte received the following letter from Maître Duforréril, her solicitor at Dieppe:

"MADEMOISELLE,

"I have just received your telegram asking me where we stand in the matter of our enquiries. I have already given you the information which I obtained regarding your life and that of your parents at Liverpool, although this, unfortunately, told us nothing new. M. Kellner, which was the name under which your father made his fortune at Liverpool, left none but pleasant memories behind him in the commercial world of that city. On the other hand, no one knew anything of his private life or of his antecedents.

It was not even known that he was married; and this fully bears out what you told
me of the retired existence which your
mother and yourself used to lead.

"I was therefore obliged to pursue our
investigations to Berlin, which takes us six
years further back. Your father at that
time called himself M. Dumas. And here
we have evidence that a fire broke out on
the 15th of October 18— in the warehouse
of M. Dumas, a bonder of Anjou wines,
in the Frischwasserstrasse. Among the
rooms completely destroyed was that which
M. Dumas, who was at the same time a general agent, used as an office in which to see
his clients, most of whom were countrymen
of his own. M. Dumas made an affidavit
from which it appears that all his papers
were burnt.

"On this side, consequently, we arrive at
a very unfortunate certainty: your family-
papers are no longer in existence; that is
clear. We have therefore to trace your

parents back to the time of their departure
from France.   Once we have done this and
discovered the town in which they used to
live, it will be easy, by advertising, to find out
who you really are.

"Your father had in his employment, in
Berlin, a Frenchman of the name of Renaudeau, whom he appears to have trusted absolutely and to have treated, according to
the neighbours, as a friend of long standing.
When he left Berlin, he made over his business to Renaudeau.   Next year, Renaudeau
went bankrupt.   But he is believed to be at
Hamburg.   I have written to the French
consul there; and I will let you know as
soon as I hear from him."

Day after day went by, days like those
which followed on her arrival at Domfront.
Gilberte once more became the recluse to
whom none had access save the poor and destitute of the countryside; and, though they
still spoke of her as *la Bonne Demoiselle* of

the Logis and blessed her for her charity,
it might well be that they no longer took
away with them that impression of comfort
which they welcomed no less than the alms.
How could she have consoled them, she who
herself was yearning for consolation?

However, she did not give up all hope.
Gilberte had one of those rather passive natures which, in happy hours, overflow with
generous gladness, but which, at times of
trial, fall back upon themselves and live in
that kind of quiet contemplation which is as
it were a patient expectation. Mastering
her sorrow and checking any signs of re-
bellion or distress, she appeared less sensi-
tive than others to the most cruel blows with
which fate overwhelmed her and, through
every obstacle and every vicissitude, she pursued her inward dream, sad or joyous, bright
or gloomy, but always built up of love and
kindness.

The most appalling time was the close of
day. Night fell late at that time of the

year; and it would have been sweet indeed
to go down to the summer-house after dinner.   She had not a doubt but that Guillaume was regular in his attendance at their
former trysting-place.   He must be stretching out his arms to her now, calling her, en-
treating her, reproaching her: oh, the tor-
ture of not being able to go to him!

She never ceased thinking of him.   The
memories of their common past formed the
only charm of the present; and, by one of
love's illusions, she made her own memories
begin on the very day on which Guillaume's
began.   And so she remembered the minute
when he had caught her raising her mourning-veil in the garden by the ruins.   She
remembered the moment when, hiding behind a curtain, he had come near to her for
the first time.   Had she not always loved
him?   Why had she, from the first and despite Guillaume's deliberate rebuffs, sought
to tame him, as Mme. de la Vaudraye called
it, and to win his liking?   Why also her im-

pulse of friendship towards the mysterious unknown?

Gilberte took little or no heed of what the town said of all these happenings, having asked Adèle not to tell her: an order which the unfortunate servant found great difficulty in obeying! Domfront was bubbling and seething with comments! For, after all, there was this undeniable fact: in the sight of the whole world, as everybody could bear witness, a formal proposal had been made for Gilberte's hand in marriage; and it resulted in a breach between the La Vaudrayes and Mme. Armand. A complete breach! For they no longer even saw one another. And the inexplicable thing was that, since that famous afternoon, Mme. Armand had not once left the Logis.

What was underneath it all? From which side did the breach come? A score of contradictory versions went the round of the town, but none of them bore the marks of indisputable authenticity upon which the

ever-scrupulous world insists before accept-
ing a piece of gossip as fact. As for Mme.
Duval, she was in a desperate plight.
Pressed with questions, she was reluctantly
compelled to admit that she knew nothing.

After the first fortnight, Gilberte, who
dared not walk in her garden, ventured to
go out once or twice, but only at times and
in directions where she ran no risk of meeting people. Generally in the early morning, she would slip out by a side-door and
make her way down to the river by the most
shady and roundabout paths of the wood
skirting the Logis.

Her almost daily destination was the little chapel of Notre-Dame-sur-l'Eau. It
was here that she had had her last interview
with Guillaume. It was a peaceful spot,
where she loved to dream. One day, when
she was coming back by a rambling way, she
passed the house which was once tenanted
by those Despriols who had brought about
M. and Mme. de la Vaudrayes' ruin. The

rusty bars of the gate seemed crumbling to pieces. A tangle of weeds and brambles overran the garden. The front of the house was cracking; the slates of the roof were green; the windows were full of swallows' nests. Everything spoke of desertion and neglect. Nevertheless, Gilberte felt drawn to it.

The gate resisted her efforts and she walked round the garden-wall, feeling sure that she would find a door near a corner which she saw a little way off. She did find one; and it was open, as was the door at the top of the steps leading up to the house.

She had no sooner gone inside than the impression which the old house had made upon her became so distinct as to awaken recognition. It was that curious impression which we sometimes receive in the presence of scenes which we are sure that we have never looked upon and which nevertheless we seem to have always known. It is impossible that we should ever have visited a certain town; and yet the street in which we are is quite familiar to us: we have seen this shop before, that sign-board, this gable, that turning.   Where and when?   In what bygone existence?   Or is it only an illusion awakened in our brain by a series of similar pictures?

"This is the drawing-room," said Gilberte, before opening the door.

And she amused herself by likewise pointing out, with absolute conviction, the kitchen and the dining-room.

But her astonishment was great indeed when, on the first floor, she entered a large room hung with grey wall-paper, on which birds and butterflies flitted amongst blue flowers.   Where had she seen those flowers, those butterflies, those birds before?

She gave a start: in a corner, on the dusty floor, lay a doll, the last stranded relic of all that had once filled the house.   And Gilberte knew that doll, knew it beyond a doubt.

She picked it up and, at the first touch of

it, was seized with an extraordinary emotion,
as though it had been a doll of her childhood,
a doll with which she had played at the age
of three or four, one of those dolls which
little girls treat as babies, lavishing on them
all the devotion, the infinite care, the tender-
ness, the pride and the anxiety of the future
mother.   And she saw this one, this poor,
wretched rag of a doll, with no clothes and
only half a head, she saw it, or rather recalled it, clad in a dress of orange silk and
a green shawl, with bronze shoes on its feet,
a silver chain round its neck and the most
wonderful mop of yellow hair upon its head.

She held it for a long time; and it seemed
to her that her hands were used to that
clumsy body and to the badly-jointed arms
and legs.   Nothing about the doll disgusted
her.   She felt as if she could kiss the little
porcelain forehead, the prim, painted eye-
brows, the chubby cheeks.

There was a faint sound behind her.   She
turned round and saw a dirty-looking woman

with curiously staring eyes and great wisps
of white hair all round her head.   She was
showing her teeth in a fixed and silent laugh.
On the linen rag that did duty as a necker-
chief hung a queer necklace made of chips
of glass, pebbles, corks and twisted grass.

Suddenly the face became contracted with
rage: its owner had caught sight of the doll.
She ran up to Gilberte, snatched it from her
hands and brandished it as though she would
have struck the girl with it.   But the doll
fell to the ground, the threatening gesture
ended in an attitude of hesitation and the old
woman, with her body bent forward and her
eyes staring, gazed at Gilberte.

Gilberte was frightened at first, but became gradually reassured under this steady
gaze in which she seemed to feel an ardent
and curious affection.   She smiled at the
old woman, who gave a silent laugh, picked
up the doll and handed it to her humbly and
gently.   Gilberte refused to take it and the
old woman grasped her hand and led her to

the second floor, to a cupboard crammed with child's shoes, rattles, broken toys, a little cradle, a chair on wheels and showed them to her with an air of saying:

"Pick where you like, take what you like; I give them to you."

But none of these things tempted Gilberte. Then the old woman took her down to the garden, led her to an acacia-tree, to a wooden bench, to what remained of a dovecote and, at each halt, questioned her with her eager eyes.

At last, Gilberte felt weary; little by little, since the woman's arrival, the deserted house had lost its mysterious charm for her; and she began to think of going. Thereupon the old crone, anticipating her wishes, took a key from her pocket and opened the rusty gate. She stooped, as Gilberte went out, and kissed the hem of her dress.

Turning round, a few minutes after, Gilberte saw her standing in the middle of the road, making signs to her.

When she returned to the Logis, she told her adventure to Adèle, who exclaimed:

"Why, it must have been Désirée, the Despriols' old nurse! She is a poor old madwoman, but quite harmless, and lives near Notre-Dame-sur-l'Eau. She does nothing but wander round the house where she was a servant. She has been mad for quite two years, ever since the death of her husband and her three sons. It came upon her all of a sudden . . ."

"But had the Despriols a child?" asked Gilberte.

"I should think so! A little girl who might have been three or four years old at the time when they went away: a dear little duck; and her nurse adored her. It broke the poor thing's heart to part with her. Since she went mad, she thinks oftener of the baby than of her own three sons. They did say that she heard about the child and that Mme. Despriol used to write to her."

"Did you know this Mme. Despriol, Adèle?"

"That I did, at Mme. de la Vaudraye's, when they lived here. . . . She was a very nice lady, so cheerful and pleasant; good-looking, too, but, worse luck, so weak with her husband that he did as he liked with her."

"Mme. de la Vaudraye told me something about some jewels . . ."

"Oh, that was quite true! There's no denying it: a thief she was . . . and Mme. de la Vaudraye has good reason not to love her. And how she does detest her! And then she was jealous of M. de la Vaudraye, who ventured to flirt just the least bit with Mme. Despriol. You can imagine how mad Mme. de la Vaudraye was! She turns pale to this day, if you mention Henriette Despriol's name . . ."

A few days later, Gilberte received another letter from Maître Duforneril:

"Mademoiselle,

"We are making headway with our enquiries and I hope soon to send you the news of our success. This Renaudeau who took over M. Dumas' business in Berlin is, as we thought, at Hamburg. He has seen the consul and declares that he knew your father for many years, going back to the date when he was still living in France. He refuses, for the present, to reveal M. Dumas' real name and antecedents; but I have no doubt that this Renaudeau, who is in a state of the greatest poverty, will yield to certain arguments.

"I think I may safely say, therefore, that my next letter will inform you of the name of your parents and the place at which you were born. . . ."

XI

GILBERTE'S NAME

GILBERTE, who was less proof against joy
than sorrow, awaited her solicitor's promised
letter with feverish impatience. Another
four or five days, a week perhaps; and the
mystery would be cleared up and the only
obstacle to her marriage swept away.

She kept more and more indoors. What
was the use of short, stealthy walks, when
her imagination, which was now unfettered,
took her across the immensity of the world,
on Guillaume's arm, under Guillaume's
eyes? She tried to read novels, to calm her
excitement. But what are fictitious adventures worth at a time when our own destiny
is on the point of fulfilment and when it is
to be fulfilled in cloudless happiness? The
one and only adventure was that which was

leading her towards Guillaume.   The story began and ended with Guillaume.   Guillaume was its sole hero.

"It will come to-morrow," she said, each day, with the fixed intention of sending the letter, the moment she received it, to Mme. de la Vaudraye.

The morning came and the afternoon and brought no letter.   She felt not the least disappointment:

"It will come to-morrow," she thought, all a-quiver with hope.

The postman became a person of importance in her eyes, a gentleman worth considering.   She shot her prettiest smiles at him, as though she were trying to win his confidence and to persuade him that he must have a letter for her in his bag.

Adèle was enraptured:

"Oh, ma'am, you're becoming as you used to be!   And high time too!   Yes, I was growing uneasy at seeing you always sad, taking no interest in things and looking so

pale. But, there, you're right: there's as
good fish in the sea as ever came out of it!"

Released from her silence, Adèle was at
last able to repeat all that Domfront had said
about the breach and all that was happening
now. And Gilberte learnt that Mme. de la
Vaudraye's *salon,* after closing for three
weeks, had reopened. M. Beaufrelant and
M. le Hourteulx had been invited. Mme.
Duval even predicted an approaching recon-
ciliation with the younger Simare, whose
father had never ceased pleading in his
favour. At the last reception, the duet from
Mireille, as sung by M. Lartiste the elder
and Mle. du Bocage, both of whom were
making great progress, had been vigorously
applauded. But the chief thing was the
transformation undergone by Guillaume,
whom everybody considered changed for the
better.

"They can't get over it," said Adèle. "I
hear that he is the life and soul of the party
and so amiable and so polite: just like a

proper young man.   He seems on the best of terms with his mother.   The young ladies are all gone on him.   Bless my soul, he's a good-looking lad . . . and it won't take long before he's turned all their heads . . ."

Gilberte reflected:

"He's quite right to make himself amiable. It's the only way to get round his mother."

Nevertheless, she had to make a certain effort to look upon this as the only explanation of Guillaume's conduct.

Two more days followed without a letter. Then, one morning, Adèle came back from her shopping:

"Here's a bit of news!" she said. "There's no harm in telling you, now that you've got over things.   M. Guillaume is engaged to the eldest Charmeron girl."

Gilberte burst out laughing:

"It's one of Mme. Duval's matches!"

"No, no, I hear it from others as well: the Bottentuits' servant told me; so did M. Beaufrelant's gardener.   Mme. de la Vaudraye announced it last night when every one was there."

Not for a moment did Gilberte admit the possibility of so great a perfidy. Nothing evil could ever come from within her: no suspicions, no doubts, no base thoughts; and whatever came from without broke against her love like impotent waves. How could she have pictured treachery, who did not know that treachery existed?

She was therefore very cheerful all day long. Nevertheless, at sunset, an irresistible force drew her to the ruined summer-house. Guillaume was not among the rocks in the valley.

Nor did she see him the next day. That night, she had a touch of fever and her mind wandered a little, mingling the picture of Guillaume with that of Mlle. Charmeron.

She laughed merrily at all this on waking. Nothing could touch her faith in her lover. She was as sure of him as of herself.

She rose in good spirits, resolved to be

happy come what might. And she was
happy: a plucky creature judging others by
her own lofty standards, whose nerves and
woman's instinct may be alarmed for a moment, without allowing a breath to disturb
the serenity of her soul.

She played and sang until lunch-time.
After lunch, she strolled in her garden and
picked some flowers. When she went in,
she found Guillaume waiting for her in the
drawing-room:

"You . . . you . . .!" she murmured,
half-swooning with emotion.

She was obliged to sit down and they remained at some distance from each other, not
daring to raise their eyes. It seemed to Gilberte as though her whole life would not be
enough to take in all the joy that wrapped
her round. How right had she been to be
happy in spite of all things and to prepare
herself for this greater happiness, which she
could never have borne, had she been sad and
suspicious.

Guillaume asked:

"Did you not meet my mother?   She is looking for you in the garden."

"Is your mother here?"

"Oh, Gilberte, would I have come without her, when I would not even go over there, among the rocks, for fear of displeasing you?"

She recalled her disappointment of the last evening and the evening before and was on the point of accusing herself . . . but of what?   Had she lent a willing ear to the calumnies of the town?   She said, simply:

"I am glad of what you have done for Mme. de la Vaudraye."

"What have I done?"

"Was it not a sacrifice to be at her parties?"

He went up to Gilberte:

"A sacrifice?   Not at all. . . . Ah, that's because you don't know what has happened during the last few days! . . . Why, I am prepared to do all that she wishes and to take an interest in all that interests her and to like everything that she likes! . . . If you only knew, Gilberte. . . . Listen . . . or rather, no, I prefer that she should tell you . . ."

"Oh," cried Gilberte, "if they are hopeful words, precious words, why not say them yourself, Guillaume? Will they not be sweeter if I hear them from your lips? Speak, Guillaume . . . I want them to be associated in my memory with the sound of your voice . . . please, please . . ."

She besought him with her gentle, loving smile.   He at once said:

"Very well, Gilberte, I will."

He was interrupted by Adèle, bringing in a letter on a tray.   Gilberte took the letter and, while the servant was leaving the room, mechanically cast her eyes upon the postmark.   A cry escaped her:

"Guillaume!"

Her fingers trembled.   She could only whisper:

"A letter from Dieppe . . . from my
solicitor. . . . Oh, I was waiting for it so
anxiously! . . . Think, Guillaume: it brings
me a name . . . nothing can separate us
now . . ."

The excitement was too much for her.
She felt herself small and feeble in the grip
of an over-great happiness. And, covering
her face with her crossed hands, as was her
wont at moments of perturbation, she wept
tears of delight.

Some minutes passed in silence. She
heard Guillaume open the garden-door.
Steps approached, some one sat down beside
her, a hand unlocked her fingers: it was
Mme. de la Vaudraye.

She shrank back imperceptibly. But
Mme. de la Vaudraye said:

"Gilberte, are you afraid of me?"

And the voice was so gentle that Gilberte
was quite stirred. She looked at her
through her tears and hardly recognized her.
Her features had lost their customary hard-

ness, her countenance the expression of implacable pride that deprived it of all its charm. And this charm now showed itself in the eyes, which had lost their severity, in the pathetic wrinkles of the forehead, in all that sad and withered face.

"Gilberte, you wished to be my daughter: do you wish it still?"

She had no time to reply. Guillaume had rushed up to both of them and was kissing them by turns. And he said, fervently:

"Let us love her, Gilberte. We owe her the greatest gratitude for what she is doing. It means the sacrifice of her most cherished ideas and she has consented to that sacrifice of her own accord."

"Come, Guillaume, don't make me out better than I am!" protested Mme. de la Vaudraye, in a playful tone. "Are you quite sure that I have not merely yielded to sordid motives? If Gilberte had been a poor girl, without any money . . ."

"Oh, madame," said Gilberte, "that counts for so little!"

"Yes, with you and Guillaume, who are young and think only of your happiness, but not with me, who have suffered so much from the change in my fortunes. I can't help it: one cannot alter at my age; I have a name of which I am very vain; and my dream has always been to restore it to all its brilliancy."

She playfully stroked Gilberte's hair:

"And think of all my blandishments, from the very beginning, Mme. Armand! You can't say that I wasn't clever in getting round you and making you do what I wanted! Well, then, one day, you tell me that you have bought up my family estates and you offer to reinstate me as mistress of the Logis. How could I have the courage to refuse?"

She displayed a sort of unspoken wish to make amends to Gilberte, a wish which her pride prevented her from revealing as openly

as her heart would have prompted her, but
which, nevertheless, appeared in her manner of confessing, as though in fun, the
shabby side of her behaviour.   Gilberte had
too much delicacy of mind to take pleasure
in this admission and replied:

"It's your son's happiness which you have
not had the courage to reject.   It is so easy
to tell that all your ambitions and all your
hopes are only for him."

But Guillaume was less indulgent and exclaimed:

"Really, mother, one would think that
you were trying to cheapen your consent!
Come, tell her of our talks of the past fortnight, tell her that you know the whole story
of our love and that you understand Gilberte, as she deserves, and that that is why
you agree."

Mme. de la Vaudraye made a last stand.
It was the final effort of her vanity.   She
seemed undecided, bewildered, staggering,
like one trying to keep her footing before

falling; and then, suddenly vanquished, she took Gilberte in her arms:

"Yes, child, yes, it was you who conquered me . . . I have come to you not because you are rich and generous, but because you are good and sincere and the noblest creature that ever lived. . . . Yes, I have thought of the future, from the start, and I think of it still; but, also from the start, your goodness has been working on me as on every one else. I loved you apart from any sort of calculation. And, after refusing my consent, it was no use my heaping up reasons to confirm me in my resolve: I could only remember your dear gentleness, your innocence, your childlike simplicity."

"Oh," whispered Gilberte, "how happy you make me!"

"You shall always be happy, child, where it depends on me: that I promise you. . . . As for Guillaume, oh, if you knew how he speaks of his sweetheart! I know you now as well as he does. But did I need his words in order to know you?   What he feels in you, that delicate bloom and innocence, I have always felt.   And I know all the power of your eyes: they bring purity and peace . . . one is better for looking at them . . . one sees more clearly . . ."

Gilberte, in her confusion, nestled her head against the friendly shoulder.   She was delaying, as a joy in reserve, the news of her recovered name; and the thought of the pleasure which she held in store gave her tiny thrills of impatience.   She said, in a whisper:

"Then . . . my name . . . my past . . ."

"Rubbish!" cried Mme. de la Vaudraye. "What did all that matter where you were concerned, my innocent Gilberte?   Those prejudices fade away into nothing when we look at them with your eyes and judge them with your candour."

"Do you mean that?" asked the girl, releasing herself and looking at her with a radiant air.   "Have you no regrets?"

"None at all."

"Then read this letter, which has just come: it will tell you the secret . . . I too have a family. . . . Ah, madame, you will have no need to blush for me!"

Mme. de la Vaudraye did not at first understand; then, when Gilberte had told her of the search conducted by the solicitor, she could not conceal her satisfaction:

"So you have succeeded? Oh, I am glad! . . . Why should I deny it? I was bothered in advance about what other people would say: pardon my weakness, I can confess it now that I have accepted you as a daughter before knowing that your parents were worthy of you. The fear that they might not be was the only obstacle; and that was irrevocable. But I overcame that fear. Something to boast of, was it not? As though it were difficult to know them, when one knows you!"

She took the letter, felt it and said:

"We shall soon learn the name of two

good people. Your father must have had your fascination, Gilberte; and your mother: I picture your mother as an exquisite, charming creature like yourself. . . . Did you love her very much?"

"More than my life, madame."

"Here, Guillaume, read it out."

Guillaume took and opened the envelope. As he was unfolding the letter which it contained, he had a momentary hesitation.

"Why, what's the matter?" asked Mme. de la Vaudraye.

"Nothing," he said, presently.

And he unfolded the letter.

They were there, all three of them, affected in different ways, but anxious and even a little timorous, as we are at the approach of the solemn events of our lives, even when we expect nothing from them but pleasure and satisfaction.

"Well?" asked Gilberte, who was certainly the least excited of the three.

Guillaume made up his mind and read, aloud:

"MADEMOISELLE,

"As I expected, our friend Renaudeau did not persist in his silence very long and, without further procrastination, has told us as much of your father's story as interests you. We now know that, at the time when he was living in France . . ."

Guillaume stopped. He hesitated once more and the letter fell from his hands to his knees.

Mme. de la Vaudraye grew impatient:

"What are you thinking of, my boy?"

He replied, in a dreamy voice:

"I am thinking that we are about to violate the secret of two persons who must surely have had their reasons for keeping it so carefully. They may have been the offspring of two rival families, or a pair of lovers who were kept apart by convention,

but whose hearts drew them together.   Who
can tell?   In any case, don't you think that
their secret belongs to them and that there
is no reason that authorizes us to violate
it?"

"What do you mean?"

"Oh, mother, tell me what reasons you
can have, tell me before that angel who is
listening to us!   You treated them as rubbish just now: have they become graver reasons since?   State them: express your fear
of public opinion, your dread of evil tongues,
your horror of comment; and, as you do so,
look into that pair of child-eyes and ask
yourself if they understand what you are
saying."

She protested feebly:

"What   a   strange   wish,   Guillaume!
There is something which you are keeping
back."

"Yes," he cried, rising from his chair,
"there is something else which I do not see
clearly. . . . It is my love that objects. . . .

I don't want to lift the veil that shrouds Gilberte. . . . I prefer her so. . . She is more mine like this . . ."

He was walking up and down excitedly. Gilberte held out her arms to him. He flung himself on his knees before her:

"Gilberte, I beseech you, remain for me the dear unknown whom I loved from the first day that I saw her. I do not know what prompts me to beg this of you, but I want you to give me the intense joy of feeling that you exist only through me, that you are commencing your life with me, that you are heaping still more darkness upon your past so that your eyes may be obliged to turn still more towards the future. Be the unknown lady of the Logis. Be the unknown who mingled her dreams with mine, the dear unknown who came from I know not where, but who came to me, of that I am certain."

She hung on his words. He stammered, incoherently:

"Oh, you will do it . . . I feel it! . . . And yet, Gilberte, listen . . . the secret is yours . . . you yourself have the right to know . . ."

She answered, with a smile that lifted him into the seventh heaven:

"Guillaume, I do not want to know what you will not know. . . . Besides, it matters so little! I was only happy for your mother's sake."

He bent his head and kissed her hands. Presently, they heard Mme. de la Vaudraye tearing up the letter. She said, simply:

"It shall be as you wish, my dear children. But don't you think, Guillaume, that there will be difficulties, that the law requires . . . ?"

"Never mind the difficulties!" he cried. "We shall see to that later. Everything will be settled as we intend, I am sure of it."

A long silence followed, full of grave sweetness. At the end of it, however, Guil-

laume, smitten with a vague remorse, murmured:

"And so, dearest, you will never know
your name?"

She smiled:

"But I know my name: is it not Gilberte
de la Vaudraye?"

"But your mother?"

"Oh, my mother!" she said, with shining
eyes.   "Mother's name was mamma!"

THE END